BONANZA

BONANZA

Killer Lion

Authorized Edition
based on the well-known
television series

by STEVE FRAZEE

illustrated by
JASON STUDIOS

WHITMAN PUBLISHING COMPANY • Racine, Wisconsin

Printed in U.S.A. by Western Printing
and Lithographing Company
Racine, Wisconsin

CONTENTS

1 Running Shot 7

2 The Captive 19

3 A Terrible Mouser 41

4 Skunked 58

5 The Cave 76

6 Desperate Journey 97

7 Farewell 117

8 The Ponderosa 130

9 Nocturnal Visitor 144

10 The Killing 163

11 Caught! 186

12 Treed Lion 200

1

Running Shot

FROM THE CORNER of his eye Hoss Cartwright caught just a flash of movement up on the tumbled rocks below the rimrock of Horse Thief Ridge. He checked his big sorrel horse, Paiute, and squinted through the thickly falling snow.

Movement. That was all he had seen. It could have been some small animal scooting toward its den, or perhaps even a bird winging along under the projection of the overhanging stone. Now he could see nothing up there but rocks that were turning wet brown as the snow struck and melted.

Anxious to get back to the stable at line camp on

Two-bit Creek, Paiute rattled his bit rollers and looked around at the rider as if asking why they were stopping in the middle of a storm.

For several moments Hoss continued to study the rocks. He was a big, good-natured man who looked even larger than he was because of his bulky sheepskin coat and huge gray hat.

There might be a wolf den up there, and if there was, he'd better know about it. It was getting on toward spring, when a mother wolf would have hungry pups. Both she and the male would be pretty busy hunting—mighty bad customers to have in the same area as the herd of whiteface cows Hoss had been watching for the last month.

When the storm ended, maybe he'd just better go up there and search those rocks thoroughly.

The wet snow was beginning to make his hat brim droop. Paiute stamped his feet restlessly and tossed his head, but Hoss waited a few minutes longer before starting on toward the cabin.

There were all kinds of animals up here in this

wild, rough country, most of them harmless. On the whole, Hoss was fond of wild things. While his brother, Little Joe, and his father, down at the Ponderosa, would likely laugh their heads off at him if they knew, Hoss had got about half friendly with an old mother skunk who had a den with five little skunks somewhere near the line cabin.

Why, with a little more encouragement those doggone baby skunks would have been all over the cabin, but Hoss had been careful not to let the friendship develop quite that far.

Still keeping one eye on the rocks, Hoss directed Paiute along the edge of the aspens. It was the first time he had come back from the herd by this route. Generally he used the trail much lower down, but today he had used the shorter way in an effort to get to the cabin before the storm grew too intense.

For a month he had been watching a small bunch of Herefords Pa had bought that winter. They were a new breed to the Ponderosa. Before buying any more of them, Pa wanted to know how they would stand up under tough range conditions.

In a few more weeks it would be Little Joe's turn to come to line camp and Hoss could go home.

Suddenly Paiute stopped. He snorted, then tried to run downhill into the trees, and Hoss had to rein in hard to get him under control.

"Easy, boy, easy," Hoss said soothingly.

Something was up there in the rocks, sure enough, and Paiute had got a whiff of it. As a colt the horse had almost been caught by wolves. He still had a tendency to spook at the scent of them, and sometimes even dogs made him nervous.

It was only natural that Hoss was thinking of wolves as he dismounted quickly and pulled his rifle from the boot. He tied the trembling horse to a tree. Snow melted on the weapon as he levered in a cartridge and let the hammer down to safety.

He went slowly toward the cliffs, studying the openings among the huge granite slabs. It would be pure luck if he got a crack at a wolf in this terrain, but at least he might get some idea of where the den was so he could come back later and clean it out.

He moved slowly, carefully. The wet ground absorbed most of the noise of his boots. The light was poor for shooting, and he knew that any chance he got would have to be taken quickly and offhand.

Pushing his way through the gloomy hollows of the rocks and through tangled brush, he came to a narrow place that made him uneasy. He had never known of a wolf attacking a man, but any kind of savage animal with young could be dangerous when crowded.

Ahead of him lay a maze of passages. He realized that it would take the best part of a day to search the jumbled rocks. Now the snow was beginning to stick, covering the ground instead of melting. All view of the slope below him was cut off by the great rocks.

It was already late in the day, and the storm made it seem even later. Hoss went slower and slower, picking his way, stopping frequently to listen. He came to a place so narrow that he knew he would have to squeeze through it sideways. He backed away from it and climbed the sloping side of the rock.

Now he could look back and see Paiute. The horse was not watching him, but was intent on something farther west along the cliffs. Hoss knew he could trust the animal's vision far better than his own, so he took his lead from the horse and studied the cliff that had caught the attention of Paiute. But all that Hoss could see was snow falling on grim rocks. He decided not to go any higher. He might stumble around close to the wolf den without finding it, and that could scare the mother wolf into moving her pups to another den that he would never find.

With one hand he shook the snow off the collar of his sheepskin. He looked back and observed that Paiute was still alertly pointed, head high and ears pricked forward.

Squinting through the storm, Hoss stayed where he was for a few minutes more.

He was turning to leave when he saw it—up

there, just below the broken face of the cliff! A long, tawny form seemed to flow through the air as it went from one rock to another.

A mountain lion!

Hoss had raised his rifle the instant he caught the first sign of motion, but in the same instant the big cat had gone from the top of one rock to another and then disappeared.

He put the weapon to his shoulder, waiting. It seemed that a long time passed, and nothing happened. Doggone tricky cats! That's the way it usually was—you saw a glimpse of them and then they hightailed it, keeping out of sight. That lion could be a half-mile away by now.

Still Hoss waited, tense and ready. He could see the tops of two small pines close to where the lion had dropped from sight. Farther on, the cliff slanted out, bare and exposed. If the big cat had gone downhill among the rocks, which was likely, all chance of seeing it again was long past.

But if it was still there and tried to escape along

the ledge of the cliff, it would have to cross that bare place. Just time enough for one quick shot, Hoss figured.

He heard a dead limb snap behind him as Paiute moved, but he didn't dare take the time to look to see if the horse was breaking loose.

The light was failing rapidly now. In about ten minutes it would be gone.

"Maybe it has a den up there," Hoss thought. In that case, it was just a mite late to be trying to roust it out. After the storm ended, when there would be tracks in the snow . . . that was the time to come back.

Hoss was just about to leave when he got his chance. The lion bounded into the open place. Hoss had about three seconds to make his shot.

As he pulled the trigger he knew it was a good one.

His bullet caught the lion in midleap. It crumpled on the ledge, then threshed for a moment before rolling limply downhill and out of sight.

"Got him!" Hoss yelled.

Though he was anxious to see the result of his shot, he took his time working his way through the rocks. It would be foolish and dangerous to rush up carelessly on a wounded animal, especially a lion.

It was almost dusk when, from the top of a rock, he looked down on the big cat.

There seemed to be little doubt about its being dead, but still he approached it carefully, ready to shoot again if he had to. It was the biggest doggone mountain lion he had ever seen. He wished Pa and Little Joe could see it.

And then Hoss saw something else. The dead lion was a female, and she had been nursing cubs.

Banging his hat against his leg to shake off the snow, he shook his head in disgust. Now he would have to return and find the den and kill the cubs, or else they would starve to death. Like any cattleman, Hoss hated lions, but he couldn't bear the thought of helpless little animals starving.

He started back to Paiute. Then, unexpectedly,

in a little opening where two scraggly pine trees stood, he saw the cub.

It had climbed one of the trees until it could go no higher, and there it had sprawled out in the puny limbs, hanging on for dear life with everything but its tail. As Hoss looked up at it, one of the limbs bent and the cub had to scramble and clutch the trunk with one paw to keep from tumbling to the ground.

Hoss lifted his rifle and sighted on the cub's head. All fuzzed with snow, the furry little face peered down at him, with one ear up, the other drooping. Once more the limbs bent and the cub made such a comic picture clawing for support that Hoss had to grin.

Doggone if it wasn't a cute, clumsy little varmint, having such a dickens of a time hanging on to that tree.

Well, it might be cute now, but cub lions soon grow into big cats—the natural enemies of deer. And calves. And colts.

"Dad-burn it, little cat!" Hoss said. "I've *got* to shoot you. And the sooner, the better."

He almost pulled the trigger. Then one of the small limbs broke, and the cub nearly fell before it got all four feet against the trunk. The tree swayed and the cub looked down at Hoss with a foolish expression.

With a disgusted shrug Hoss lowered the rifle.

"Why'd you have to be up a tree?" he growled. And such a miserable little tree, at that. If the cub had been running on the ground, trying to escape, it would have been different. Then you didn't have to look at it and start thinking. All you had to do was shoot and the whole business was finished.

Snow was falling heavier, and darkness was not far away. It was over a mile to the cabin, and Hoss remembered that he was going to have to saw stove wood. He should have done it that morning, but it had been such a fair day when he left the line camp that he thought he would have plenty of time for the chore after returning.

He had wasted enough time talking to a no-good mountain lion cub.

Quickly he raised the rifle. This time he wouldn't even think about it.

2

The Captive

IN SPITE OF his determination, Hoss Cartwright *did* think about it. No matter if that furry little devil in the tree was going to be a killer someday. He couldn't bring himself to blow it apart, not with it all helpless and small and lop-eared, looking down at him that way.

Why, the doggone thing hadn't even snarled or spit at him, come to think of it. Of course, it had been pretty busy just trying to cling to the tree.

He couldn't just walk off and leave it, what with its mother dead over there in the rocks.

He leaned his rifle against a rock and took off his

sheepskin. Spreading the garment with the fleece side up, he held it out and stepped close to the tree. He raised his foot as high as he could and drove it against the trunk.

The tree bent and then snapped back, and the cub came sprawling down and hit the sheepskin with a thump. Hoss wrapped it up, then found he had a struggling, growling little demon on his hands. He worked the coat around until the cub's head was out, and then it stopped fighting.

With the bundled lion under one arm, Hoss went back to Paiute. The horse had trampled the ground considerably, but he had made no serious effort to break loose—not until he got a whiff of the cub at close range. Hoss caught the reins as Paiute tore free and was pulling back to turn and run.

"Whoa, doggone you! It's just a little old cub."

Big or little, the odor was all the same to Paiute. Hoss had a time of it settling him down. He knew it was the better part of discretion not to try to go aboard with the burden he was carrying.

Hoss walked and led the horse back to line camp. Paiute evidently thought it was bad enough to have a lion at reins' length. Ginger, the spare horse, came out from the lean-to-stable, trotted through the corral and up to the gate—and then he got a whiff of the cub.

With a loud snort Ginger wheeled out through the open gate and went down into the fenced pasture, kicking his heels high. If he hadn't known it before, Hoss realized now that he had bit off a chunk of trouble when he didn't pull the trigger over there by Horse Thief Ridge.

He turned Paiute loose, taking the chance that the horse wouldn't go any farther than the corral gate. Paiute trotted over to the bars and then looked back to see what Hoss was going to do with that bad smell.

Hoss took the cub inside and turned it loose in the one-room cabin. It crouched on the floor, its tail switching, then scrambled away and went under Hoss's bunk.

"A good place for you, you little stinker." Soaked from the snow and tired from walking, Hoss put his sheepskin back on before he went out to take care of Paiute. Ginger came back to the stable, but when he caught the scent on the coat, he snorted and galloped back down into the pasture.

"I must be twenty-seven kinds of an idiot to pick up a lion cub," Hoss told himself. "Now that I've got him, what am I going to do with him?"

He sawed wood by lantern light, standing in the falling snow. That, too, was the dad-burned little lion's fault, Hoss grumbled to himself. When he pushed through the doorway with his first armful of wood, he heard a thump as the cub jumped off his bunk and ran back to the dark corner under it.

"You'd better stay off that bunk. You ain't going to be here very long, young fellow, so I don't want you getting familiar! Understand?" Hoss lit the lamp and kindled a fire.

The cabin was tightly built of aspen logs, well chinked and daubed with clay. It had one small, four-paned window near the table, good rat-proof cupboards, and a few items of rough furniture made from hewed logs. It was a comfortable enough place, though it did get a mite lonely during the winter evenings.

As soon as the fire began to warm the room, Hoss took off his wet shirt and stood close to the stove. He heard the cub scratching at the logs in the corner under the bunk, and then the sound stopped.

Later, making supper preparations, Hoss had to go down to Two-bit Creek for a bucket of water. When he returned he expected to find the cub roaming around the room, seeking an escape hole, but everything was silent.

Hoss knelt with the lamp at floor level and looked under the bunk. The cub was curled up in the corner, his eyes enormous in the light as he blinked sleepily at Hoss.

"Well, I'll be doggoned," Hoss muttered.

He put condensed milk into a pan, mixed it with warm water, and set the pan on the floor near the bunk. Then he went ahead and prepared his supper.

It was about an hour later when the cub stirred. Hoss was lying on his bunk when he heard a slurping noise. He looked down and saw the cub lapping the milk, his whiskers and muzzle wet with it. The man watched him quietly.

Something sure had happened to that one ear; it was crumpled and misshapen, as if it had been half chewed off. And then Hoss saw something else. Extending from the shoulder down the cub's right leg was a furrowed wound. It appeared that he had been raked hard and deep. The injury was healing, but the hair had not yet grown back.

The cub got his muzzle too deeply into the milk and choked. He growled at the pan as if it had attacked him, then backed away and went under the bunk.

Twice during the night the cub roused Hoss. Once he heard it lapping milk. The other time it was playing with the cinch ring of one of the saddles across the room. In the morning when Hoss woke, the cub was sitting on the table, sniffing at the window.

"Get off there!" Hoss commanded.

He guessed it was the sound of his voice, rather than the command itself, that sent the cub scurrying under the bunk.

Fourteen inches of snow had fallen and more was coming. Hoss stood in the open doorway looking out at the snow, and his first thought was that he would have to cut wood again. While he was blinking at the fresh, white world outside, the cub charged past his legs and leaped toward freedom.

It landed in the snow and sank almost out of sight. After a few wallowing efforts to go somewhere, it fought its way back to the dry area under the overhang of the porch roof and shook itself vigorously.

There was little snow under the eaves close to the cabin wall. The cub raced around the corner. Hoss stepped over to see if it had landed in the snow again, and while he was looking around one corner, the cub turned the corner behind him, shot between his legs, and made another run.

It was hard to say whether he was seeking to escape or just having fun. At any rate, he made three more fast circuits of the building, and then he scampered inside and went under the bunk.

Hoss guessed that he probably never would have seen him again if it had not been for the snow.

Each animal, like each person, was an individual, Hoss knew. How each one developed depended on a lot of things, but mostly on its inborn nature. It just could be that this lion cub wasn't quite as wild and treacherous as Hoss had always thought all lions were.

He supposed the cub was associating the dark, safe place under the bunk with the den where it had been born. Its brothers and sisters might be entirely different. One of them, given a chance to escape, might have gone out into the deep snow and kept right on fighting it until exhausted.

"Rimrock, it looks like you know when you're well off," Hoss said with a laugh. Then he thought, "Rimrock. That's as good a name as any for the little cat."

After breakfast Hoss put more milk in the pan, and then he went out to dig poles from under the snow. There was plenty of wood in the pile of rich pine logs dragged in the previous fall, but it always turned out that he never had enough cut into stove lengths. This time he intended to stock the cabin with enough to last a week.

Each time he carried an armful into the cabin to stack against the wall, he eyed the pan of milk. It was going down, sure enough. Rimrock was working on it between Hoss's trips with the wood.

Long before Hoss had all his fuel cut and stacked, the milk pan was empty.

It seemed to Hoss that Rimrock was a mite big to have been nursing. He didn't know a great deal about the care and feeding of young mountain lions, but judging from the size of Rimrock, the cub should have been catching small game for himself for some time, Hoss thought.

Since making his impulsive decision to take the cub alive, Hoss had had plenty of time to think about it, and he knew he had not been very smart. Making a pet of any wild animal just didn't work out in the long run. They always grew up, and then you had big trouble.

He recalled that Corley Frakes, over on the Five Bar A ranch, had brought home a motherless fawn one spring. It became a great pet of the Frakes kids for two years, and then it turned into a fair-sized buck with horns, with a disturbing tendency to try out its horns on horses and unwary visitors.

One day it gored Corley while he was in the stable leaning over the oat bin. Soon after that the deer disappeared, and Corley told his kids it must have wandered away.

The thing to do, Hoss told himself, was to take care of Rimrock until he could fend for himself and then take him a couple of miles from the cabin and turn him loose. Like as not, by the time he was able to catch a rabbit or something of that size, he would leave by himself anyway.

Above all, a man had to keep himself from becoming fond of a pet. That's where he trapped himself.

"I'll sort of take care of him for a while," Hoss thought, "the same as I would for a stray horse, say, and then I'll kick him out and there won't be any problem about parting with him."

Hoss figured that Rimrock had gone to sleep under the bunk after drinking the milk. The general habit of lions was to prowl at night and sleep in the daytime.

And then he saw the cub come out of the cabin and run around it, batting at the snow, twisting and jumping awkwardly.

Paiute and Ginger knew he was there. They stood at the corral gate, craning their necks and blowing clouds of vapor from their nostrils.

It stopped snowing shortly before Hoss carried in his last armload of wood. He had planned to go back that day to the cliffs to search for the lion den, but now he decided it was more important to check the cows.

Rimrock was inside when Hoss prepared to leave. He blocked the cabin door part way open with a stick of wood before he left.

The Herefords had moved over toward Gold Park. They were pawing snow down to the long dead grass below and doing well. That's what Pa had wondered about, whether or not they were a breed that could fight weather and take care of themselves. Pa would be pleased to know that a little snow didn't cause them to bawl helplessly and start drifting downhill.

Hoss rode around the herd slowly, checking them, looking for any sign of weakness. He looked, too, for any evidence that predators had been near the herd.

"Predators!" he thought. "Oh, man! If Pa knew that I'd taken up with a mountain lion, even a cub, he'd hit the ceiling."

Well, Pa wasn't ever going to know about it. And neither was Little Joe, who would have plenty of sly remarks to make if he ever found out. Hoss could just hear some of his brother's smart digs about saving a lion instead of shooting it.

By the time Little Joe arrived with supplies to last him through his turn in line camp, Hoss would have Rimrock weaned away from milk and out on his own.

That reminded Hoss about going back to Horse Thief Ridge to look for the den. Of course, it might not even be in that area. Maybe the old lion had been taking her cubs out for a hunting lesson a long way from home; then, too, perhaps Rimrock had been the only cub she had.

That last didn't seem likely. Lions generally had more than one offspring.

Hoss decided to make the search the next day.

Though Hoss would never know, he need not have worried about any other cubs. There had been only two in the litter, born in a den two miles from where he had shot the lioness. One day while she was hunting, they had been rolling and playing in the sun on the shelf outside the den, a brother and sister with almost identical markings.

Locked close together in mock combat, they were growling and pawing at each other when a great shadow fell on them suddenly.

Air boomed through the feathers of enormous wings, and the powerful talons of a mother eagle, who also had hungry youngsters to feed, drove down with terrible force. One plunging talon ripped through Rimrock's ear and went on to score deeply into his foreleg.

The sharp, curving hooks of the other foot of the eagle struck into the neck of Rimrock's sister. As Rimrock scrambled to his feet one of the buffeting wings knocked him rolling. He got up again and scrambled into the den, hiding in the deepest, darkest corner he could find.

He never saw his sister again. All he knew was

that something terrible had happened.

When his mother returned, she searched through the rocks for a day and night, calling for her missing cub, and then she gave up, sensing that it was gone forever.

She had more milk then than she needed. Consequently, Rimrock nursed much longer than he would have normally, and he developed very little hunting skill when his mother tried to teach him to kill small game.

Hoss did not stay long with the herd. He had an uneasy feeling about what might be going on at line camp. When he got there, he found his hunch was justified.

Rimrock had expanded his exploration of the area. By following the trail Hoss had broken to the woodpile and on to the corral, the cub had tried to visit Ginger.

Without the presence of Hoss and Paiute it had been too much for Ginger. He had knocked a panel of poles out of the pasture fence and headed at full speed for the Ponderosa.

Hoss saw Rimrock's whiskered face peering at him from the doorway. "You did fine!" the man said with sarcasm.

He didn't dismount. If Ginger got to the Ponderosa, someone would start for line camp at once to see what the trouble was. Hoss couldn't let that happen. He set out to find the horse.

In the lower reaches of the land, where the snow began to thin out, Ginger had slowed down. He had stopped to forage here and there, though still headed for home. Hoss was ten miles from the cabin before he caught the runaway.

All the way back to line camp a bitter wind blew in Hoss's face. It was nearly dark before he got the fence patched up.

When he went inside, his foot struck something that rolled. He fell with a jarring thump. Rising, he stumbled and almost crashed down a second time. The sticks of wood he had stacked so carefully all along one wall were scattered everywhere, and the tin utensils he had left under a flour-sack cloth on the table were all over the floor.

He saw Rimrock rolling on the bunk, grabbing at the pistol belt that hung from a nail in the logs.

"You've had a real good day, haven't you?" Hoss roared.

The cub jumped down quickly and ran under the bunk.

"You'd better hide!" Hoss said.

Straightening up the mess after he got a lamp lit, Hoss saw Rimrock peering at him cautiously. Every time Hoss growled something at him the cub retreated, but he always edged out from under the bunk again to see what was going on.

"Dad-burned little varmint." Hoss muttered with a crooked grin.

When he poured milk in the pan after supper, Rimrock was ready.

"Learn pretty fast, don't you? Well, let me tell you something. There ain't many cans of this here

milk left, so you're going to have to change your eating habits pretty fast."

Sleeping soundly in the middle of the night, Hoss roused when something struck the bed. For a moment he was too sleepy to realize what it was, and then he heard a scratching on the tarpaulin as Rimrock tried his claws.

The cub tramped around, pushing with his feet, and then he curled up and went to sleep at Hoss's feet. "Well, I'll be doggoned," the man muttered. The little stinker was making a purring noise.

As soon as Hoss opened the door in the morning, Rimrock bounced outside. This time he did not leap headlong into the snow, but sat on the step a moment before racing around the cabin. Hoss walked toward the corral. He had no desire to ride after Ginger again.

When Rimrock thought he, too, should go to the corral, Hoss drove him back by throwing snow at him. That business with Ginger was a serious problem. He decided that from then on he would ride

Ginger and leave Paiute, who was not nearly as spooky about the cub.

Hoss went in to get breakfast. Rimrock was tearing the wood down again.

"Hey!" Hoss slapped him on the rump and the cub ran to his hiding place.

A few minutes later he was on the bunk, and then he was back on the floor, licking the empty milk pan.

"You're too big to be drinking milk," Hoss said. "We got to have an understanding, you and me. You may be a pretty cute little varmint, but you're still nothing but a lion. You get to hang around until the snow melts, but starting tonight, you're going to be eating meat, see? And pretty soon you're going back to the rocks, understand?"

After breakfast, Hoss gave the cub his milk.

"I ain't running no dairy here, and you'd better get that through your little flat head," he told his eager guest.

Slopping the fluid greedily, Rimrock got his nose

in too far and sneezed. He rocked back on his haunches and looked startled. When he finished the milk, he put one paw on the edge of the pan. It flew up and hit him in the face.

Hoss roared with laughter as Rimrock ran under the bunk.

3

A Terrible Mouser

THAT DAY Hoss searched for a den in the area below Horse Thief Ridge, but he found no evidence of one anywhere along the cliffs. He was glad of that, for if he had turned up another cub or two, he would have had to kill them.

One cub was enough. Maybe too much.

Ginger thought so. He didn't even like the odor of lion on the sheepskin Hoss wore.

That night Hoss changed Rimrock's diet. Meat was the natural food for a lion, and Rimrock had better understand that fact right now.

Hanging on a crossarm between two trees in

back of the cabin was a side of beef that stayed frozen in the deep shade where the sun never touched it. Hoss hacked off enough for himself and the cub.

Rimrock liked it fine and ate it readily, but he still wanted milk afterward.

"You don't act like a common, ordinary lion," Hoss complained. "No milk." He hung the pan on a nail on the wall. Then he had to hang it higher because Rimrock kept batting at it, making it swing like a pendulum.

By being extra watchful Hoss managed to keep Rimrock away from the corral for several days. He hoped that Ginger would grow somewhat used to the lion, at least enough not to crash out through the pasture fence again if the cub came close.

And then one day it happened.

Hoss had returned from riding Ginger to the herd and had turned him loose in the pasture after giving him a bait of oats. Cutting some of the last of the dwindling supply of beef behind the cabin, Hoss saw Rimrock stalking toward the corral.

"Come back here!" Hoss yelled, but it didn't do any good.

Both horses were in the corral. Paiute stayed there, though he retreated to the stable, where he turned to watch Rimrock warily. Ginger trotted down into the pasture. The horse looked like fair game to the cub, so he slipped between the fence rails and made a magnificent charge through the two or three inches of melting snow that remained on the ground.

"Whoa!" Hoss yelled in desperation, but Ginger was off at full gallop, with Rimrock, tail high, doing his best to keep him going.

Hoss was already seeing aspen fence rails breaking like matchsticks.

Then all at once Ginger turned and came back toward the cub. Rimrock plowed to a stop. Ginger stopped and sized him up from a distance. After all, the cub was not a very big thing, even if he did smell like a lion, and Ginger wasn't alone; he had Hoss and Paiute close by.

Ginger seemed to decide he had had enough of

that pesky lion. He reared up, pawing the air, and then he slammed his front feet into the snow and made a thundering charge.

Rimrock kicked snow with all four feet as he ran for safety. Belly low and tail no longer high, he shot under the corral bars just as Ginger came pounding up to the gate. The cub didn't stop until he was in the cabin and under the bunk.

Hoss was gasping with laughter when he went inside. Rimrock peered out at him cautiously.

"Ain't you the ferocious one!"

From then on Hoss had no more worry about Rimrock stampeding the horses. The cub avoided the corral. He wriggled uneasily every time Hoss carried him down to the gate to let the horses see how harmless he was.

It amazed Hoss to see how quickly Rimrock became downright tame. He was naturally playful, like all young of his kind, and in a short time he was ready to romp and roughhouse whenever Hoss had time for him. He took correction well, too. Whenever he got into mischief, Hoss gave him a spank with his hand. Rimrock would then leap up on the bunk and study the situation, determining how soon it would be safe to jump down and get into a different kind of mischief.

Though Hoss didn't think about it, he was using the same method Rimrock's mother had employed to train her cubs—a good, sound cuff when they did something wrong.

The last of the snow melted, and that was the time Hoss had set to get rid of the cub. Still, it wasn't spring yet by a long shot. There would be more bad weather, so Hoss thought it best to keep Rimrock around until he was sure the cub could take care of itself.

He sure was a smart little cat. And that lopped ear gave him a comical look. His ripped leg was nearly healed, but it would still be a while before the hair grew back to cover the angry-looking scar.

It was sort of nice to have something around the cabin to talk to. Rimrock wasn't just any old lion you could find in the rocks. No, sir! He was way out of the ordinary. Why, he seemed to understand about half of what Hoss said!

In the library at the Ponderosa, Hoss had read the story of Marco Polo and had learned how Tartar khans went hunting with a leopard crouched on a leather pad behind the saddle. When the rider saw game, he gave the word and the leopard would leap off and go after it.

Hoss guessed that even if he tried he could never train Rimrock to do that for two good reasons. First, the cub was now more afraid of horses than they were of him, and second, he wasn't showing much development as a hunter.

Rimrock's appetite was enormous. After the beef vanished, Hoss had begun to kill deer, shooting only young bucks that had come through the winter in good condition. Rimrock enjoyed the meat, but he showed no tendency to go after it himself. Rabbits were plentiful in the grass and willows along Two-bit Creek, Rimrock's favorite prowling place.

He saw the rabbits all right—sometimes they almost ran over him—but all he did was show great interest in them and let them run.

"You're supposed to be a good hunter," Hoss said. "What's the matter with you?"

Smaller game was more to Rimrock's liking. He hunted field mice industriously, pouncing on them in the grass and then snuffling them out from under his paws. Sometimes they weren't under his paws after the pounce, and this always astonished him, but still he caught his share. He ate some of them, though more often he brought them to Hoss in triumph, as if to say, "See what I caught!"

"You look like a lion, Rimrock," Hoss told him. "Dad-burn it, you *are* a lion, so why don't you start acting like one and catch something big enough to help support you?"

If there was one thing that the cub hated, it was the camp robber birds that Hoss fed with biscuits. At first, Rimrock had shown fear when their shadows fell on the ground close to him, but later he made determined charges at them when they lit beside the biscuits.

He never came very close to getting a bird, but he tried.

Ever since the cub had been at the cabin Hoss had seen nothing of the mother skunk and her little ones. It was just as well, he thought.

Hoss decided that perhaps hunger would induce Rimrock to catch something bigger than a mouse. For two days he gave the cub nothing to eat. He had no sure way of knowing if Rimrock caught anything while Hoss was away on his daily trips to the herd, but the cub didn't act as if he had done any hunting during Hoss's absence.

He rubbed against the man's legs and pawed at him and sat looking at the cupboard, where there were still three cans of milk, and sniffed wistfully while Hoss was eating. Hoss couldn't stand it. At the end of the second day he shot a rabbit and laid it in front of the cub.

Rimrock showed considerable interest in it, sure

enough. He rolled it over with his paw a time or two, smelled it thoroughly, and then he pulled its tail off.

"Well, that's a start," Hoss said hopefully. He went into the cabin. Rimrock followed him, carrying the rabbit. He put it down at the man's feet. When Hoss went to the creek for a bucket of water, Rimrock again followed him, still carrying the rabbit, and then he trailed Hoss back to the cabin and put the rabbit at his feet once more.

"I'm not going to skin it for you!"

But Hoss did. He not only skinned the rabbit, but he also cut it up—and then Rimrock ate it. Afterward he wanted milk. Feeling defeated, Hoss gave him milk.

"Doggone you, didn't the taste of that rabbit give you any ambition?" Hoss asked.

The next day Rimrock went back to mousing, while the rabbits hopped around, completely safe.

Before he went to sleep that night, with Rimrock already snoozing at the foot of the bed, Hoss tried to think things over logically. If he kept providing all Rimrock's food for him, the cub would never learn to do anything for himself. He was just like people in that respect.

Rimrock needed to be shown how to support himself, that's what. How would a mother lion show a cub how to get along, so she wouldn't have to spend all her life hauling home food for him? Simple. She would train him to hunt.

The very thought made Hoss feel sort of foolish, but since there was no one around to see him, he decided to give it a try in the morning.

Right after breakfast he took Rimrock down to the thicket of grass and willows. The cub bounced along happily. He was a gawky youngster, mostly legs and ears, but he was already showing promise of developing into a tremendous cat.

"Now, the sneak-up is the first thing," Hoss told him.

Rimrock seemed to understand. His good ear cocked forward and his crumpled ear, as usual, lopped crookedly. He looked ready for anything.

Hoss crouched low and moved slowly. Since he had only two feet, he made only about half as much noise as a big steer. Rimrock got the idea. He moved along with his belly close to the ground. They flushed out a rabbit that went hopping away between the clumps of willows.

"Get him!" Hoss yelled, and he charged.

Rimrock was with him. He stayed with Hoss even after the man fell over a hummock and went sprawling on his stomach with the wind knocked out of him. Where the rabbit went, neither of the hunters knew.

Hoss rolled over slowly, gasping for breath. Sitting beside him, Rimrock gave him a look of sympathy and licked his face with a tongue that felt like sandpaper.

As Hoss got up slowly, he saw Paiute and Ginger watching from the corral. They seemed to be giving him the horselaugh.

Rimrock made a sudden leap and pinned down a mouse. At least he made a good effort, though the mouse wasn't there when he lifted his foot.

There was only one thing left—get rid of the cub. This foolishness had gone far enough. Put him out in the wild, really out on his own. He was big enough to make it, but if he refused to learn, that was his hard luck. Why, if this hand-feeding him went on long enough, Rimrock would never amount to anything.

Kick him out or shoot him.

Hoss knew he would never do the latter.

Though Paiute had come to tolerate Rimrock on the ground, and even when Hoss held him up to be sniffed at the corral gate, the horse was dead set against having him in the saddle with Hoss.

The horse bucked all the way across the yard, through the willows, across the creek, and halfway up the little meadow beyond. Rimrock squalled and dug his claws into the man's legs, and all Hoss could do was take it and try to get Paiute under control, which he finally did. On the way to the herd Paiute cut loose twice more, but with less energy each time.

Hoss found the whitefaces a half-mile east of where they had been the day before. On the ridge above the little park, he put Rimrock on a high stump.

"You just look around and see what you make of things," he said and then waited to see what the cub would do.

One thing Rimrock grasped at once—those big red things down below looked dangerous, a whole lot like the Ginger monster that had tried to stomp him. With one eye on them he leaped from the stump and slipped away into the trees.

The last Hoss saw of him, the cub was moving pretty fast, going toward the area where Hoss had found him.

It was settled. And it was the best thing. Of course a man grew attached to a pet—even a no-good lion. It might be a little lonely for a day or two, not having anything to talk to around the cabin, not seeing Rimrock playing with the ball of rabbit fur and rawhide that Hoss had made for him.

Dad-burn it, it was the only solution. Just *feeding* the little varmint had been a problem.

Hoss knew he would shoot the next full-grown mountain lion he encountered. He had to. But if it happened to be, say, about a year from now, he guessed maybe he wouldn't want to look at it too closely afterward for fear it would have a lopped ear and a scarred shoulder.

After he left the herd, Hoss took a swing down toward Old Mine Park. He was out of meat again, but one more small deer ought to last him until Little Joe came up.

How long would that be? Come to think of it, he had been forgetting to mark the days off on the calendar. Too busy with Rimrock. Well, that problem was behind him.

He jumped a bunch of deer in the oak brush, picked out a yearling, and got it with one shot. He cleaned the deer, slung it behind the saddle, and went on back to the line camp. In spite of knowing that Rimrock was gone for good, he half-expected to see the cub frisking around the cabin, waiting to come and rub against him and *browr* a greeting as soon as Hoss got away from the corral.

While he was cooking deer liver he scowled at the calendar on the wall. He must be two weeks behind with his marks, maybe longer. A fine thing when a man lost all track of time because of fooling with a lion cub, a born killer, an enemy.

After he ate, Hoss found the cabin unusually quiet. He saw Rimrock's ball of fur and rawhide on the floor and he kicked it behind the stove. No use arguing, he had been a downright fool to bring the cub here. Nothing but trouble from then on. It was a good thing he was gone.

It was dark by the time Hoss got around to washing the dishes. He opened the door to throw out the dishwater. The lamplight fell on a gangly, furry, lop-eared animal sitting on the step.

"Rimrock!"

Rimrock *browred* and stalked inside, where he sat down and began to clean the mud off his feet.

He had traveled a long way from where Hoss had last seen him, for there was no mud that high up, but his appetite proved that he hadn't done any successful hunting. He ate five pounds of meat and wanted more.

"Now, look here, you glutton, I'm going to have to do something about you." Hoss sighed.

In the days that followed, he found out what it was he had to do: kill more deer.

4

Skunked

AMONG OTHER THINGS that proved Rimrock was no ordinary lion was his reversal—for mountain lions, that is—of day and night. He slept when Hoss slept, and in the daytime he prowled the willow thickets or the trees, or romped in front of the cabin.

For a while Hoss had kept the door closed at night, but he soon grew tired of having to get up just at dawn every morning to let the cub out. Rimrock's way of rousing the man was to walk on him, punching with his paws and making *browring* noises.

Hoss fell into the habit of leaving the door ajar so

the cub could go out and come in as he pleased. He even did this when he was away at the herd or hunting. The cub had learned that there were certain things in the cabin he must not disturb, including the firewood and the utensils on the table.

The man hoped that the cub would be brave and alert enough to rout any stray visitors that tried to enter the cabin, including rats or other rodents, though he was not sure that Rimrock would be able to turn back a determined invasion of rabbits, if that highly unlikely event ever occurred.

One early morning sometime close to dawn Hoss was sleepily aware that Rimrock had just jumped back on the bed after being out. A little later Hoss began to rouse for some strange reason. He sniffed, then he took a deep breath through his nose. That time he got a full charge of it.

Skunk!

There was a skunk in the cabin. Hoss started to leap out of bed, but on second thought he decided to stay where he was. That mother skunk with the little ones—sure as shooting, she had walked in with her whole family.

Hoss reached down and grabbed Rimrock. He didn't want the cub to leap down among the invaders and make matters even worse.

As it was, the odor was overpowering, choking.

The man's eyes rolled wildly as he peered from the bunk, trying to locate the source of trouble. Early light was coming through the window. He could make out dimly everything in the room. There didn't seem to be any white-stripers around now.

They had walked in, and then they had walked out again, for which Hoss gave thanks. And then he had a horrible thought. What if they had gone under the bunk?

He let go of Rimrock and leaned over slowly to look beneath his bed. His left hand, the same one that had grasped Rimrock a moment before, was now close to his face. A great truth struck him—and something else, too. He gasped.

Rimrock! There was the source of the odor, right

there on the bed! The cub had investigated a skunk, and a mighty close examination it must have been.

Blinking and coughing, Hoss staggered outside.

For four days and nights he wouldn't let the cub inside. He thought the exile might even cause Rimrock to do some hunting by night, to learn to be a lion, and to go away for keeps. It did not work.

Rimrock scratched at the door. He *browred* pitifully to be let in. He clung to the logs and peered in the window, looking like an abandoned orphan. At night he jumped on a broken stove that leaned against the cabin wall and went from there to the dirt-covered pole roof, where he tried to dig his way inside.

One night he got clear down to the bare poles and pawed loose the dead grass and moss that had been stuffed between them. Dirt came streaming down, and Hoss found the table a mess in the morning.

And then one night, as Rimrock jumped down from the roof after a digging session, he overturned the broken stove. The frantic squalling that ensued brought Hoss out of bed in a rush. He found Rimrock with his tail caught under the edge of the stove, digging and yowling for all he was worth.

When Hoss freed him, Rimrock raced into the cabin and got on the bunk.

Hoss gave up. Anyway, the worst of Rimrock's odor was gone. "Or maybe," the man told himself, "I'm getting so used to it I can't smell straight."

Watching Rimrock yawn and stretch one day, Hoss suddenly realized that he wouldn't be a cub much longer, not the way he was growing. He was already three times as big as the pathetic little animal Hoss had shaken out of a tree.

He *should* be growing, the way he was eating. But to the man's knowledge, the biggest game the cub had killed so far was still a mouse. It was awful.

"If you'd just go after rabbits as ferocious as you charge them camp robbers, you'd get somewhere," Hoss told the lion, but Rimrock ignored his advice.

Curiosity and friendliness, that was old Rimrock.

He got so he tried to make up with the horses. Ginger would have nothing to do with him. Given a good chance, Ginger would have stomped him three feet wide and two inches thick. Paiute, however, reached the point where he would lower his head and sniff without alarm when Rimrock sat just outside the corral gate, trying to be friendly.

Previously the cub had been content to stay somewhere close to the cabin when Hoss was gone, but one day he decided to follow the man and Paiute. Hoss had to dismount and send him home with a few cuffs, and then Rimrock got on the cabin roof and watched him out of sight.

Though Hoss had not marked his calendar for a long time, he knew that Little Joe was due before very long. Maybe Rimrock would take up with Little Joe, and then. . . . It was a thought, but not a good one. Little Joe would kick like a steer if Hoss tried to unload the burden of getting rid of the cub on him.

It was Hoss's responsibility to return the lion to

the wilds. He'd always known that, right from the first day he carried Rimrock to the cabin. He decided to lose the cub, to take him so far from line camp that there would be no question about it.

Hoss put his plan into effect early the next morning. Paiute accepted Rimrock without bucking too much this time when Hoss took the cub aboard. Hoss rode west for about seven miles, then five miles north toward Signal Peak. It was ideal lion country —rimrock, big trees, and small parks where deer were plentiful.

Without dismounting, Hoss put Rimrock on top of a huge granite block.

"So long, you lummox." He turned Paiute and rode away.

The cub didn't try to follow. The last Hoss saw of him, Rimrock was investigating a badger hole.

All the way home Hoss kept watching for the lion. He made a long detour, just in case Rimrock was following off to the side and not directly behind. Lions were famous for that kind of trailing, drifting as silently as smoke beside whatever they were following.

Hoss cut back and forth across his own trail several times, and twice he went back to search on both sides of where he had been riding. There were no tracks.

The slow riding, his detour, and all the other stratagems used up a lot of time. It was late when he reached the cabin.

He was dead right. Rimrock had not followed him through all the devious twisting on the way home, but had gone straight back to the cabin when it pleased him to do so. There he was, waiting at the door with an expression that seemed to ask, "What took you so long, Hoss?"

The man had a sneaking suspicion that the cub had been there for hours.

"You're not going to get away with it!" Hoss warned.

Rimrock stretched. He scratched the door.

That night something happened which gave Hoss

a faint glimmer of hope that Rimrock was growing up. The sounds of a terrific battle brought Hoss from sleep. He heard thudding, growling, squealing —sounds of a fearful combat being waged near the pile of wood along the wall.

Hoss grabbed his pistol.

The uproar had ended by the time he got a lamp lit. Rimrock had killed a rat. Not a very large one, but a rat, nevertheless. In the process he had scattered the firewood all over the floor again, but he had won the fight and he was proud of himself.

He put the kill at Hoss's feet and Hoss praised him for his courage and daring, but when the man threw the rat outside and Rimrock brought it back and laid it at his feet again, Hoss yelled, "I ain't skinning no rat for you!" Once more he threw it out.

In the morning it was back on the floor by his bunk. Hoss found that out when he put his bare foot down on it. There is nothing like stepping on a dead rat to make a man jump and yell. Rimrock was startled to hear such a bellow from his master.

Hoss solved the problem by burning the rodent in the stove.

His hope that Rimrock might get ambitious as a result of his conquest of such big game and go on to better things seemed to be soundly based, for later that morning Hoss looked out and saw Rimrock stalking a rabbit with deadly intent.

The rabbit was feeding near the edge of the willows. Using all available cover, Rimrock was closing in on it with the masterful motions of a lion stalking its prey. Even if he didn't get it, the idea at last was in his head, Hoss thought. Rimrock was showing some signs of responsibility!

Close to the ground, his tail quiet, the cub made a classic sneak, moving only when the rabbit wasn't looking. And then Rimrock charged.

The charge consisted of two big bounds and then a jump straight up in the air, after which Rimrock sat down and watched, while the rabbit, not unduly alarmed, hopped back into the safety of the thicket.

Hoss closed his eyes and groaned. His expression was painful to behold.

In desperation and in spite of his previous failure to instruct Rimrock in the art of hunting rabbits, he decided to try again. His faith in the idea was not too strong, as evidenced by the fact that he strapped on his gun belt.

He took Rimrock to the lower end of the thicket, just above the beaver dam. They worked the edge of the willows. Again Rimrock got the idea. He inched along alertly as Hoss tried to do the same.

The same careless rabbit—or maybe another who knew Rimrock—came from cover and began to browse farther and farther from the willows until he was dangerously exposed. One rousing charge could cut him off from safety.

Man and lion leaped forward, and, sure enough, Rimrock was able to keep the rabbit from getting back into the willows. The rabbit had to go into the open, toward the cabin, where Rimrock's great short-range speed gave him all the advantage.

But his speed lasted only so far, and then he leaped straight up into the air and sat down.

In frustration Hoss tried a shot. He was not nearly as proficient with a pistol as he was with a rifle. The shot proved that. The bullet struck behind the rabbit, sliced off the frozen ground, tore a hole in the cabin door, and carried inside to cut an ugly rip in the skirt of Hoss's best saddle.

"I'm going to quit teaching you anything!" Hoss yelled. "You're the dumbest lion I ever met!"

That was the day Rimrock followed him to the herd. Hoss noticed that Ginger was edgy, but he did not realize the lion was following until he was ready to go back to the cabin. Then he saw Rimrock sitting in the trees, waiting.

From then on Hoss was never able to break the lion of the habit of trailing him.

On the way home Rimrock loped along in front of Ginger as boldly as you please. Ginger tried twice to overtake him and hammer him into the ground. The first time the horse almost unloaded his rider in a thicket of wild roses, and the second time he took Hoss through some low limbs that knocked off Hoss's hat and snapped him briskly across the upper lip.

Hoss was carrying his saddle into the cabin when he saw Rimrock grow tense, sniff the air, and then scoot inside. Moments later Hoss heard the sound of horses. Little Joe!

But it was not Little Joe. Hoss was outside, with the door closed, when he saw the riders make the turn at the beaver pond. Sam Hargis, who had a ranch east of the Ponderosa, and two of his cowboys, Slim McCrea and Kansas Weber. A lean, dark-faced man, Hargis was a good neighbor, though he was a mite ornery and set in his ways at times.

Thinking about Rimrock, Hoss greeted the three men. They dismounted and stretched their legs.

"We've been scouting around all day east of here," Hargis explained. "I lost a calf to lions last week. Worst year for lions I ever saw over where I am, but the sign sort of thinned the farther we came west.

How's it been with your herd, Hoss?"

"No trouble over this way, Sam." Hoss was sweating. Custom said he had to invite them to eat and spend the night. "I shot a female the other day, but that was the only one I've seen all winter."

Kansas Weber grabbed the reins of his horse as the animal started to wheel away. The other two horses were nervous, too. "You must have some of the smell on you," Kansas said.

"I reckon. I started to skin the doggone thing, and then I decided it wasn't worth the work."

Slim McCrea wrinkled his nose. "Had skunk around, too, I see."

"One got in the cabin," Hoss said. "It's awful in there." He took a long chance. "You boys come on in and I'll make—"

"Not today, thanks." Hargis hauled down on the reins of his horse. "Hold still there!" He turned back to Hoss. "We could put up with the skunk smell all right, but I want to get back to the camp on the Ten Mile tonight. Just that one lion, huh?"

Hoss nodded. "That's all."

Hargis shook his head. "That couldn't be the one that got my calf. He went north, as close as we could make out. Anderson lost a colt, I understand. We may just have to make a drive before long."

"Yeah," Hoss mumbled. "I sort of lost track of time up here. What's the date now?"

"It must be the fourteenth," McCrea said. "Ain't that right, Mr. Hargis?"

"Just about, I guess. You looked any farther west for lion sign, Hoss?"

"Some, yes. I didn't see much over that way, either."

"We ain't going to make it to camp before dark, anyway, Mr. Hargis," Kansas said. "Since Hoss asked us, I could stand a cup of coffee, at least."

"So could I," Hargis said. He hesitated. "No, I guess not." He got on his horse. "Yes, sir, I think we'll all have to get together before long and hire Curly Joe with his pack of dogs to clean out a few lions around here."

Kansas glanced longingly toward the cabin. He wanted that coffee badly, but he didn't argue with his employer. He and McCrea mounted.

"I'll be going by the Ponderosa in a few days," Hargis said. "Any message for your pa?"

"Just say me and the cows are getting along fine, and that I'll be looking for Little Joe. You might tell him to have Little Joe bring up a dozen extra cans of milk when he comes."

As soon as the words were out, Hoss wished he hadn't made the last request. When he and Little Joe had packed the winter supplies into the cabin, they had brought three cases of milk, and Little Joe had remarked that he would not have to bring any more when he came.

Hargis, however, didn't see anything unusual about the request. He waved and rode away with his men, and Hoss let out a big sigh of relief. Whew! That had been close. And if the ground hadn't been frozen, Rimrock's tracks would have been everywhere around the area.

No use stalling any longer about it—he had to get rid of the cub.

In four days Little Joe would be up. It was very unlikely that he would come early, not Little Joe; but he sure wouldn't be late, either.

Hoss went into the cabin slowly.

"Rimrock, we've come to a parting of the ways."

The cub rubbed against his legs and made its *browring* noise.

Four days. If he hadn't been able to get rid of Rimrock in three months, how was he going to do it in four days?

Shoot him?

Hoss knew he could not.

5

The Cave

IF HE COULD have chosen the time, Hoss would have picked a day other than the one following Hargis' visit for what he had to do. The sky was too clear and blue and there was a warmth in the air unusual for the time of year. Hoss could feel a storm in the making, but he had no choice but to go. Little Joe's date of arrival was too near to cut it any closer.

He rode Ginger, on the theory that the horse's hostile attitude toward Rimrock would help get it through the cub's head that he was not wanted.

His destination was the broken country beyond Soda Springs, twenty-some miles from the cabin.

He knew Rimrock was following, though he caught only glimpses of the cub until late in the afternoon when Hoss killed a deer north of Soda Springs.

Rimrock knew about that sort of business, all right. He came in for the feast, carefully avoiding Ginger. After that the cub followed openly all the way to the potholed gray cliffs where Hoss made camp on a wide ledge in front of a cave.

For a while Rimrock was puzzled by the campfire. He crouched some distance from it and *browred* his concern, but after a time he crept in and explored the cave. Finally he got on Hoss's blanket roll, where he felt safe, cocking his head curiously when wood popped in the fire.

He looked so much like an overgrown kitten that Hoss felt a little ashamed of what he was going to do.

Rimrock didn't sleep at the man's feet that night. Instead, he curled up in the cave, but at dawn he was out, walking up and down on Hoss to rouse him. It was still warm, but the sky was overcast now.

Hoss cooked breakfast hastily.

A snowstorm suited his purpose, but he wanted to be back at line camp before night because it was the time of year when winter's last fling could be dangerous to a man caught in the open.

"You're not going to like this, old lop-ear, but I can't help it."

To start, Hoss wedged a big rock across the narrow entrance to the cave. He set it even with the level of the deep, sandy talus and made sure by pushing on it with his foot that it would not settle any lower when undermined. Then he gathered more rocks until he had enough to block the cave opening solidly.

He let Rimrock eat all the deer meat he wanted, and then he put the cub inside the cave and sealed the entrance with the heavy stones.

Hoss didn't feel good about any part of the business. He stood for a while talking through the rocks to the cub. "You can dig out when you set your mind to it, and then you'll be in country where you belong. I'll leave the deer right here where you can smell it. After you eat it . . . well. . . ."

Hoss saddled Ginger and rode away quickly.

It ought to work. Rimrock could dig out in a hurry if he tried, but his stomach was full, so maybe it would be several hours before he got around to it. He had enough to eat for a few days. After that, hunger ought to spur him along. He wouldn't be jumping straight up in the air when he saw a rabbit; he'd be tearing after it in earnest.

Doggone it, it just had to work!

But the farther Hoss rode, the more he worried. Suppose Rimrock dug down and hit a stone that he couldn't move? What if he knocked down the rock barrier and got caught, maybe hurt bad?

Did he even know enough to try to dig his way out?

Of course he did! And there was the meat real close to give him a good reason to get out.

Hoss reined in and sat motionless for several moments, looking back. It was just beginning to snow. "No!" he thought. "I'd be a fool to go back." He rode on.

A voice mocked him. *If you don't go back, Hoss Cartwright, you'll never know whether or not you left a poor, helpless cub to starve, will you? You'll never be sure, will you?*

Hoss went over it once more. Any animal could dig when it had to. Rimrock would be all right.

In no time the snow was falling so thickly that he couldn't see a hundred feet ahead. About an hour later he began to wonder where he was. Familiar landmarks were blotted out by the storm, but he knew he was on a different trail from the one he had used in coming.

Because of the white gloom he had missed a turn where the trails forked higher up, and now he was going downhill beside a small creek that he didn't recognize. All streams in the area, however, flowed in a general southerly direction. By following any of them he would come out on the flats, and then he could orient himself.

THE CAVE

The dim game trail beside the creek was growing slick from snow. On his left was a sagebrush hill. On his right was the stream, with a dense growth of aspens. The gulch kept pinching in, the sides growing steeper, until Ginger had to feel his way carefully along the narrow trail above a chain of small beaver ponds.

The place where Ginger slipped was not as bad as some he had crossed. It happened very quickly. The hind feet of the horse slid downhill, and then Ginger started to roll. Hoss kicked free of the stirrups and pushed himself clear. An instant later the rolling horse knocked him into the pond.

Hoss went clear under. He came up gasping, chest deep in the icy water. Ginger was at the edge of the pond, on his feet, struggling to get to the dam. With one hand Hoss grabbed his hat, floating on the water. He waded toward the floundering horse, tripped over a log thrust into the mud near the beaver house, and went under again.

That was when Ginger made it to the dam with

his wild threshing. The horse tried to go over it and became helplessly entangled in the jackstraw pile of logs and brush.

Hoss reached the struggling animal and grabbed the bridle. "Easy there, boy. I'll get you out." After calming the horse, he began to tear loose the logs that had trapped its forelegs.

And then he saw that Ginger's right front leg was broken.

The trembling horse seemed to know it, too. He looked at Hoss in mute appeal. His face grim and tormented, Hoss stripped the saddle and bridle, tossing them over where the dam winged against the steep hill.

He drew his pistol and tried to blow the water from it. The first time he pulled the trigger, the cartridge misfired, and that made his task all the harder.

A few minutes later, cold as he had ever been in his life, he was tramping down the trail, carrying the saddle and bridle and his other gear. His clothing was frozen, rasping loudly as he strode along. He knew he had to keep going until the exertion warmed him a little, and then he would have to build a fire.

It was snowing harder than ever.

Where the gulch widened, with aspens growing on both sides, Hoss stopped to build the fire. He broke dead twigs from the trees and heaped them against a slanting stump that offered a little protection from the falling snow.

His pants pocket was frozen shut. He had to pry at the cloth and finally rip it to get out the cartridge shell that held his emergency matches. He saw that the wax seal was still intact.

While he was doing that, snow blew in on his pile of twigs. They did not ignite on the first try. His fingers were so stiff that he fumbled away the second match and it fell into the snow.

For the first time in his life he realized how easily a man could die from hurrying at the wrong time.

Rubbing his hands together vigorously to warm

them, he looked around until he spotted a thick clump of dead grass under a windfall. He put his kindling on top of the grass. His clothing crackled as he knelt. One touch of the flaming match ignited the grass, and in a few minutes he had a good fire going.

Now he was all right. He wasn't sure how far he was from the line camp, but he knew it was a long way. He would have to stay until he dried out, maybe until the storm ended.

His frozen clothing grew limp and then began to steam as he exposed one side and then the other to the roaring fire.

Yes, he had it beat now. He wondered how Rimrock was doing.

Rimrock had no worries. The warm, dark cave brought back memories of the den where he had been born. It was very quiet outside, but that did not bother him. He could smell the meat just beyond the rocks at the cave entrance, and that seemed to be evidence that the man he trusted so well was not far away.

The cub took a nap.

He woke up refreshed and ready to greet the man or to go with him anywhere he wanted to go. The quietness was disturbing. Rimrock pawed at the rocks. They were heavy and placed so they would not slide or tumble. He could see daylight between them, and at the bottom there was an inch or two of light in places.

Rimrock sniffed at the opening. He tried to put his paw into it. The decomposed rock and sand gave way easily. He began to dig. After a few exploratory strokes, he was pawing earth furiously. The opening became large enough for him to thrust his muzzle into it.

He tried to wedge his body through, kicking with his hind feet at the pile of sand he had thrown behind him, but he did not get anywhere. Then he sat down and waited for the man. The scent of him was still out there. Even after the snow began to cover the ledge and the dead fire site, Rimrock could smell the scent. It was on the rocks that blocked the cave, on everything that the man had touched.

It was strange that the man did not return.

The cub pushed his muzzle into the opening and *browred* several times. He pawed at the unyielding stones. He scratched the sand aimlessly in various places around the cave.

Though he was growing uneasy about being shut in—it had never happened to him before, except for a short time in the cabin—he still felt no need to apply himself vigorously to enlarging the opening by digging.

The snow continued all day and into the night. It stopped sometime during the dark hours when Rimrock was sleeping.

It was morning before he really went to work on the opening he had started. He was hungry and there was food only a few feet away.

There were others who had scented that food.

A black bear with two cubs had been prowling

the base of the cliffs since early morning. Her cubs had romped some distance from her on adventures of their own, when suddenly they had detected a tantalizing odor. In a world sparkling with a rising sun on new snow, the little bears sat up, snuffling, getting a bearing on the delightful smell.

Scrabbling for all he was worth, Rimrock forced his way outside, blinking in the sudden brightness. The first thing he saw was a magpie pecking at the carcass of the deer. Infuriated, the cub leaped at it, batting the air with his paw as the bird flew away. He shook the sand from his fur and began to stuff himself, the just desert of a great warrior who had just routed a hated enemy.

The next threat was much different. Two furry black things with a strange odor came scrambling up onto the bench. They rocked back on their heels in surprise when they saw Rimrock. He warned them off with a snarl.

For a moment it was touch and go about who was going to run. It could have gone either way, but hunger was a primary force in all three of the animals.

One of the bears inched forward and grabbed a hind leg of the deer. He didn't have anything but skin and bone, but it was his. He tugged at it, at the same time growling at Rimrock.

Rimrock leaped across the carcass and batted him in the ear, and then leaped back. The second bear joined his brother. They both moved ahead and began to eat, while Rimrock backed off, undecided. Then he bared his teeth and switched his tail.

Nothing like this had happened to him since he had jostled for food with his almost forgotten sister. He was hungry, and those two little black monsters were making hoggish inroads on *his* meat.

Rimrock leaped on the invaders, clawing and biting. He found that they could bite back. In an instant the three of them were one rolling, squalling, squealing ball of black and tawny fur. The little bears had needle-sharp teeth, and they could whack quite effectively with their paws.

Rimrock got in some excellent rakes with his hind legs and sent black fur up in little puffs. His strategy was to strike and jump back, but things went wrong. One bear nipped his front paw and the other one got him by the root of the tail and tried to chew it off.

Though Rimrock was scratching away with all his might, it was just too much when he felt himself being attacked on both ends. He broke loose and leaped away, and then he came right back and rapped his claws into the tail-biter's nose.

The cub complained loudly and at the same time tried to knock Rimrock over with a sweeping cuff with his front paw.

And then a monstrous, coughing, grunting figure charged onto the bench to protect her cubs. Rimrock took one look at the open mouth and great white teeth, at the piggish little eyes inflamed with rage.

He leaped down into the rocks and made his escape. He had now seen enough of bears to last him a lifetime.

By noon Hoss was convinced that everything he had done in the last two days could be lumped together as the biggest blunder of his life.

He had done a terrible thing to Rimrock. He would have to go back to the cave as soon as he could. The loss of Ginger was indirectly due to his getting that crazy idea about the cave, and he could lay the rest of his bad luck down to that, too.

Worst of all, he was on the verge of going snow-blind.

He had stayed all night by the fire, drying his clothing, dozing a little under the crude lean-to shelter he had made. At daylight he recognized that he was on one of the branches of Sentinel Creek, seven or eight miles from Running Bull Flats.

The shortest way back to line camp was an old cow trail through the hills, easy enough for a man on horseback, but with ten inches of snow, a man on foot was better off going to the flats and then along the edge of the hills until he struck the trail up Two-bit Creek.

Before leaving his campsite, Hoss put his saddle and bridle in a tree. He would have taken his rifle on the chance of getting a rabbit on his way home, but the stock had been broken when Ginger rolled down the hill, so he left the weapon. His sheepskin coat was still wet. It would take days for it to dry out thoroughly, so he put that on top of the gear in the tree.

Even before sunrise the glare on the snow was bad enough, but afterward it was a brilliant, burning force that shattered into his eyes and made him squint until his face muscles ached.

Before he reached the flats, he built a small fire and then used the end of a charred stick to rub black around his eyes. That was some protection from the glare, but he knew he hadn't done it soon enough.

Now he was on the flats where there was nothing to break the smashing reflection of the sun. He walked with his eyes drawn down to slits, moisture streaming from them, red flashes leaping across his vision. Now and then he stopped to rub snow against his eyes. That eased the pain some, though it did not improve his vision.

He remembered that Doc Inman, in Virginia City, had once told him that a certain quality of fluffy new snow and bright sunshine could bring on snow blindness in some men before they realized what was happening. It was an actual burning of the eyes, like a blistering of the skin from sun.

In spite of the bright sun there was little heat in the day. The temperature was dropping and a wind was beginning to ruffle the surface of the flats. Hoss knew what was coming—one of the coldest nights of the year. He had no desire to spend another night in the open, although he knew it might come to that.

In boots not built for walking he kept plodding across the blazing whiteness of the flats. Occasionally he squinted painfully at the hills on his right. As long as he guided himself by them he could keep his direction.

For a while he made good progress, but as his vision began to bother him more and more, he had to slow down. Clumps of scrubby rabbit brush were the only contrasting features in the flat whiteness, and they were growing more difficult to see. He found himself stumbling over prairie dog mounds and walking into the craters at the entrances to their burrows.

He had to move slowly, picking out a bush ahead, going to it, and then sighting on another one which seemed to be in line with the way he wanted to go. As time passed, the hills on his right became a confused dark mass. He wasn't sure that he was even seeing them. What he thought were the hills might be the darkness that was everywhere at the outer limits of his faulty vision.

If he wandered off to the left, he would be going out on a treeless waste that was five or six miles wide. He tried to keep crowding toward the hills, for he knew if he had to stop, the trees were the only refuge. With a good fire, he could last through the night there all right, he was certain.

The very thing he dreaded now happened.

He came across footprints. Snow had blown into the marks, but as he stood there, shading his eyes, blinking down at the tracks, he knew they were his own. He had gone in a circle in spite of his efforts to go from one bush to another in a straight line.

He raised his head to look toward the hills. Now he was utterly confused. He could not see the hills, and he didn't know which way he had turned when he wandered in a circle. Panic told him to run in the direction he thought was right, but he knew that a mistake now was a matter of life and death.

He knelt in the snow and studied the footprints. It was misery to his tortured eyes, and because of the snow that had blown into the trail, he could not be sure which way the tracks pointed. He crawled on hands and knees until he came to a footprint that had been protected by a bush from the blowing snow.

Facing in the direction the footprint pointed, he

extended his right arm. Over there. The hills had to be that way. It was exactly opposite the direction he had wanted to go minutes before when panic threatened.

He stumbled away. He would have to be very careful with the three matches he had left. To reassure himself he felt deep in his pocket for them. They were there, still in the cartridge case, but the wax seal had come off. He rubbed his hands on his shirt and then he carefully shook the matches into his palm.

Their heads had mushed away. Each time he had bathed his eyes with snow, he had thrust his right hand into his pocket afterward to warm it, carrying moisture. Now he had three worthless wooden sticks.

"I've still got to get to the timber," he thought.

If he could find it.

6

Desperate Journey

THE ENRAGED MOTHER bear followed Rimrock only a short distance before returning to her cubs—and the feast that someone had provided so handily for all three of them. Rimrock continued to run until he knew he was quite safe. He was then on a rocky ledge above an aspen thicket.

He stayed there for a while, licking his hurt paw and looking down at the snow in the trees. There was a vague familiarity to everything around him, but he was not satisfied. For one thing, he was very hungry.

After a time he wandered down into the aspens,

looking for mice, but he found nothing in the trees but snow. He skirted the edge of the grove and went downhill. The man must be somewhere around.

A shadow slid swiftly across the snow. Rimrock went bounding back into the trees to crouch beside a log. It was only a hawk cruising low, looking for something to eat, and Rimrock was too big for it. The cub stayed by the log until he was quite sure that the bird was no longer above him.

He heard a squirrel chattering in a pine tree, and he went over to investigate. It scolded him from the high branches, and he sat below, holding up one paw, realizing the futility of trying to catch a squirrel in a tree.

Then Rimrock caught another scent that he recognized. He traced it to a small pine that Hoss and Ginger had brushed against in passing. Rimrock sniffed all around the place. He pushed his muzzle into the snow. His tail was hurting and he was limping. He didn't know just what to do next.

He was a pathetic-looking, bewildered little lion,

far from his adopted home and the man who always took care of his needs.

The trees grew slowly out of the painful haze before Hoss's eyes. He came to an aspen and grabbed it as if it were an old friend. In the uncertain gloom farther up the hill he thought he saw a dark mass of pines. They would offer him better shelter than the leafless aspens.

He toiled uphill, slipping and stumbling. The pines, if they were really there, never came any closer. The snow was beginning to crust, and the wind sweeping off the hill was needling through his vest and shirt with fingers of ice.

Maybe later, when his eyes grew better, he would go on to the pines. Fumbling his way, he found enough dead aspen to make a crude windbreak. On the downhill side he kicked the snow away, and that was about all the preparation he could make for spending the night.

After an hour he knew it might not be enough

for survival. His tight-fitting boots were soaked, and now that he had stopped walking, his feet began to freeze. As long as he stood, stamping them to keep circulation going, he was all right.

The cold was fast becoming a crackling force. Hoss knew he had to stay on his feet, to exercise, to stay awake all night. He wondered if he could do it.

He knew he had to.

Then tomorrow. . . . If his eyes were no better, what could he do? He might be completely blind by then. Maybe it was better to keep going now, to do the best he could and try to find the cabin.

It was only about seven miles away, he estimated. Walking would keep him warm. Once again panic urged him to plunge away. Maybe he would be lucky and it would work out all right.

He knew better. If he listened to that voice, he would soon be wandering blindly, wearing himself down until exhaustion dropped him. No, he had to stay where he was, to stick it out some way, even if it took two days and nights.

His chances of surviving were not good, but there was no chance at all in frantic exertion. A broken leg—even a twisted ankle—and he would be finished.

For a long time he stayed on his feet. It was more tiring than walking. Those wet boots. . . . It would be a terrible chore to get them back on if he removed them, but he decided to do it anyway.

He took his knife and ripped his shirttail off and wrapped his feet in the cloth. Now he could keep them reasonably warm by rubbing them while he was sitting, or by wiggling his toes.

After a time he was sitting with his hands under his armpits, his head drooping toward his knees—and he was not moving.

The sound of the wolves woke him.

He staggered to his feet, thinking they were close. The long-drawn howling came clearly in the frozen night, over to his left somewhere. He could tell by the tone that they were after something, a pack of them leaping through the snow.

He was relieved when the noise faded away.

In spite of his determination to stay awake after he sat down again, he dozed. Several times he was able to rouse himself and stand up, and then when he felt that he was wide-awake, he would sit down once more. The intervals between wakefulness grew longer.

The trouble was, he did not realize how cold he was.

And then there came a time when the cold no longer mattered. Sitting there hunched over and freezing, he dreamed that he was home at the Ponderosa, warm and comfortable.

Little Joe was there, trying to make him get up and go to work, pushing at him, annoying him, making strange noises. Hoss tried to shove him away. He did not want to rise. Everything was fine just the way it was.

But Little Joe kept bothering him. The odd noise he was making became an anxious *browr*. Hoss's hand touched warm fur. Something licked his hand.

It still took several more moments for the impressions to sink into his numbed brain.

"Rimrock," he mumbled. Hoss almost slipped back into warm apathy, but the lion continued to disturb him. Finally he came awake.

"Rimrock!" he yelled. As he lurched to his feet, his body felt so stiff and wooden that he would have fallen if he had not wrapped his arms around a tree. "Where did you come from?"

The cub rubbed against his legs.

By exercising slowly Hoss brought his circulation back. For a while it took all the willpower he had to move, to stamp his feet and flail his arms against his chest. He realized then how close to death he had been.

It made him feel better to have Rimrock with him, though the cub's presence in no way made the man's position any less precarious. He had no idea of the time. The stars were out, but he couldn't see them very well. If anything, his eyes were worse than ever.

Rimrock padded around restlessly, out into the trees and back again. He liked to sleep at night himself, but the man had not picked a very good place for resting. Caves were much better, and even better than caves was the snug place on the bunk in the cabin.

Rimrock continued to walk out into the trees, standing there with a questioning *browr* before returning.

"The cabin," Hoss thought. "He wants to go home."

He began to struggle with his boots. They were frozen stiff, but he tugged and hauled and grunted until he got them on. Maybe it was a wild chance, but Rimrock had come this far, and now he surely ought to be able to find his way home.

Hoss followed him into the night.

Sometimes Rimrock went so far ahead that Hoss had no idea where he was. At such times the man stopped and called to him, and the lion always came back. Later, he seemed able to sense from Hoss's

stumbling progress that something was wrong with him, and then he stayed closer.

The route Rimrock chose was the shortest one, through downed timber, across gullies, and over rocky ridges. Hoss did not argue with it. He got up when he fell and kept on going where Rimrock went.

He lost all track of time, of the hours of groping his way up hills, stumbling over rocks and trees under the snow, and the many times he stopped, trying to peer ahead to see if Rimrock was still there, waiting to hear some sound from him.

Rimrock was always there.

Hoss never knew how long it took, for he had no idea of the time, except that it was still night, when he heard a horse nicker. Paiute!

He staggered into the cabin and gave a silent prayer of thanks. He thought briefly of building a fire, but it wasn't worth the effort. For the trip to the cave he had taken some of the extra blankets from the old metal-bound trunk in the corner, so his bed was still intact. He got into it as soon as he could undress.

For a while he was cold and shivering, but then he began to warm slowly. Rimrock's body sent heat against his feet as the cub took a well-deserved rest.

At times Hoss was aware of the pain in his eyes, but mostly he slept. He guessed it was late afternoon when he rose. He had left the door partly open as usual, and now the cabin was deathly cold. That and the fact that his eyes were worse than ever told him grimly what would have happened to him on the bleak, frozen hill if Rimrock had not found him.

He had to feel his way around. The water in the bucket on the shelf near the door was frozen solid. After he got a fire going, he put the bucket on the stove. By its shape he identified a can of corned beef in the cupboard. He fumbled the key over the tab and twisted the can open. The contents were a frozen block which he shook out into a frying pan.

Rimrock came in, demanding food.

Luckily, Hoss still had part of a deer hanging behind the cabin. He found a badly ripped black sateen shirt that Little Joe had left, and he used part of it to tie around his head, letting the cloth hang loosely over his face to protect his eyes from direct light.

The air was bitter as he shuffled through the snow to get food for Rimrock. Rather than hack at the frozen meat, he cut the rope and let the carcass fall. Rimrock promptly dragged it into the cabin, but Hoss didn't know that until he went inside and stumbled over it.

"I'll even let you get away with that."

Except for one trip to the creek for water, he stayed in the cabin the rest of the day. By nightfall his eyes had improved a great deal. It was then he discovered that Rimrock had a sore paw and a sore tail.

"You and me, we both know how to get into scrapes, don't we?" Hoss scratched the cub's ears gently. "Little Joe will be here tomorrow. Dad-burn it, Rimrock, what are we going to do?"

Everything he had tried in an effort to get rid of the lion had backfired, but there must be some way. . . . Time, that was what he needed to work things out.

There was a way to get more time, all right.

The next day Hoss was waiting on Old Mine Hill. He still had the shirt hanging down his face, and now and then he lifted it to look out on the flats. It wasn't long before he saw Little Joe's calico, with two other horses trailing behind it. Hoss rode down the hill to meet him. He expected laughter and he got it.

"You practicing to rob banks, Hoss?"

"If it's any of your business, I've got a touch of snow blindness. It comes from staying in line camp and doing the work, while some people I know loaf around home all day and go to dances every night." Hoss raised his mask to glare at his brother. "Oh! I see you smeared charcoal around your eyes."

"It's something fierce out there on the flats. You think you can ride on into the Ponderosa by yourself?"

"Ain't going to."

"What?" Little Joe swung down. He was a handsome, dark-haired young man, about half Hoss's size.

"I said I'm not going in. I've nursed those blamed cows through the worst of the winter, so I'd just as well see them the rest of the way."

"What?"

"Is that all you can say?" Hoss growled. "How's Pa?"

"Pa? Oh, he's fine. I never thought I'd see the day when you'd want to stay in line camp one more—"

"You're seeing it now! Anyway, I wouldn't want to go home and have people laughing at me for wearing a shirt over my face."

Little Joe grinned. "They wouldn't laugh half as much if you wore it all the time—over your *head*."

"That's real funny, little brother."

"How come you ran low on canned milk?"

"I was making pies."

Little Joe whistled. "Who was eating them—the horses?"

Hoss partly raised the mask. "You and your smart—" From the corner of his eye he saw movement on the hill, and an instant later he caught a glimpse of Rimrock. He had left the lion shut in the cabin. "I might have known it wouldn't work," he thought.

"What's the matter?" Little Joe asked, glancing up the hill.

"Nothing! It's just that I can't waste any more time standing around here jawing. I'm going to stay at line camp until Pa says come in, so take your war bag off that packhorse and head on back. Tell Pa the cows are fine."

"Oh, I'll do that, Hoss. Now, me, I'm not worrying about those cows in the least. It's *you* that's got me wondering what's going on. All that milk, for one thing. You raising a pet billy goat or something?"

"Seven baby mountain lions and four bear cubs. I wasn't going to tell you, but you're so smart there's no use trying to keep it from you. Now get your stuff and give me that packhorse."

Little Joe wasn't satisfied. "How come you're using that old broken-down saddle?"

"Because I had to leave mine over east of here the other day when Ginger busted his leg."

"Is that when you went snow-blind?"

"Yeah!"

"I just asked." Little Joe shrugged. "You don't have to bite my head off. What with all the bad luck you've been having, I'd think you'd want to get out, instead—"

"I'm staying, so quit arguing about it."

"All right; all right." Little Joe took his war sack off the packhorse. "Don't think it makes me unhappy. I won't have to eat my own cooking, go to bed at eight o'clock, throw stove wood at pack rats half the night in order to—"

"I've got those rats cured of bothering me," Hoss said. "After I unload the grub, I'll turn the pack-horse loose, and he ought to get back to the Ponderosa about as soon as you do."

"You want my extra horse?"

"That little thing! He'd be swaybacked in two days trying to carry me. Old Paiute and me can make out for what little time is left."

"Lions trouble you any this winter, Hoss?"

"Nope!"

"I guess they've been pretty bad over east."

Hoss eased his mask up slightly to steal a glance at the hill. Rimrock was keeping out of sight.

"You sound like Sam Hargis," he muttered. "A man would have thought old Sam had lost fifty calves, the way he was whining about lions the other day when he came by the cabin."

"Doggone, you're getting touchy! Hargis *did* lose some calves this winter, and some of the other ranchers say this has been the worst year for lions they've seen in a long time. Curly Joe and his dogs have been—"

"Did Pa say how much longer I ought to stay with the cows?"

"I think you've stayed too long already, as grouchy as you are." Little Joe shook his head. "Pa told me to use my own judgment about how long to watch the herd, so I guess you can do the same."

"Three weeks will do it. I'll come in then." The cows could be left alone right now, Hoss knew. He needed the three weeks to do something about Rimrock.

"Now that you got that extra canned milk to make pies, maybe they'll sweeten up your disposition some before you come home." Little Joe laughed and started back toward the Ponderosa.

The packhorse hated lion smell. It was on Hoss's clothing to begin with, and then there was a big bundle of it in the form of Rimrock frisking along beside the trail on the way back to the cabin.

Sometimes Paiute almost had to drag the packhorse, and at other times he had to hold strongly to keep from being dragged himself. As soon as they were close to the cabin Hoss slipped the pack, saddle and all. When he untied the lead rope from the halter, the packhorse, snorting and kicking, went back down the trail at full tilt.

He would slow down when he hit the flats, Hoss knew. Once in the open, the horse would sense that there was no danger of his being caught by a lion.

Hoss lugged the supplies inside. He had been hoping that Rimrock had dug his way out of the cabin, or had jumped against the door until the latch popped up, but no—Rimrock had gone through the window.

"You sure did yourself proud with that jump, you knothead. Now I've got to cover that hole with something, and then it'll be darker than the inside of a cow in here."

Rimrock thought the new opening was fine. He leaped up on the table and went through it, and Hoss was just a few inches short with his flat-handed swing at the lion's disappearing rump.

"I thought I had you broken of jumping on that table!" Hoss roared. He solved the problem by moving the table away from the window. When Rimrock came back in through the opening, he made a very flat landing on the floor.

Hoss laughed till his sides hurt.

Surprises were not yet over for the day. At dusk Rimrock walked in with a rabbit in his mouth.

"Good boy!" Hoss praised him. "Now you're getting somewhere."

It seemed that Rimrock did not want to progress too fast, however. He carried the rabbit around and kept putting it at Hoss's feet until the man skinned it for him. Afterward Rimrock demanded milk.

7

Farewell

THE DAY AFTER meeting Little Joe, Hoss rode through melting snow to make his delayed check on the herd. The cows were all right. Hoss knew that for all the watching they needed, he could return to the Ponderosa that day.

He had given himself three weeks more. What for? Already he had tried every reasonable move he could think of to get rid of Rimrock. The extra time wasn't going to make any difference; it would only serve to make parting with Rimrock all the more difficult.

There the lion was, sitting up on the hill as usual,

looking down distrustfully at the cows. He wouldn't come within two hundred yards of them. Hoss wasn't sure, but he had a sneaking suspicion that maybe Rimrock was afraid of deer, too, on the hoof, though he was certainly a great admirer of them on the platter.

But there was hope in the fact that Rimrock was expanding his skill at catching rabbits. Although Hoss still had to skin them for him, he kept telling himself that it was really a big thing that the lion could even catch them.

Why, old Rimrock had even made a pass at a beaver from the pond below the cabin. The beaver had stood its ground, showing its long yellow teeth. Rimrock had hesitated at the last moment. In fact, he regressed into his old habit of jumping straight up in the air and then sitting down.

It was a good thing, though, a smart move. The beaver was pretty close to the water, and no animal in its right mind wanted to tangle with a beaver in the water. Come to think about it, that straight-up jump had been about the prettiest one Hoss had ever seen Rimrock make.

Hoss looked the herd over carefully. He back-tracked through the melting snow to where the cows had bunched up in a dense juniper thicket during the cold spell. No one could say *they* were dumb.

Rimrock joined Hoss in the junipers.

"Well, did you learn anything about being a lion today?"

Rimrock sat down and scratched behind his lopped ear. On the way home he was very bouncy, and when they reached the cabin he bounced right through the piece of rotten canvas Hoss had nailed over the window.

The man hung an old saddle blanket over the opening, fixing it firmly at the top and letting the bottom hang loose. Rimrock could then whisk back and forth through it as he pleased.

"Everything around this place is run to suit you," Hoss complained.

Rimrock's sociability reached a startling new

high point the day he went with Hoss to recover the gear Hoss had cached in the tree. The snow was almost gone then; the sun was bright, and it was a great day for riding—and it turned out that Rimrock was in hearty agreement with the last thought.

Hoss retrieved his gear. He changed saddles, tying the old one behind him, with his sheepskin on top of it. For a while he rode along the edge of the flats. Rimrock stuck to the trees and rocks of the hills. Like any lion, he was wary of exposing himself in daylight in open country.

When Hoss cut back to the trail that led through the Holcolmb Hills, the lion was with him. He was very much with Hoss as the man rode past an outcrop of rock.

As Hoss passed, Rimrock jumped on the gear behind him.

"Hey!" Hoss tightened the reins. He expected a barrelful of fireworks from Paiute.

Nothing happened. Paiute took the incident in his stride.

"I'll be doggoned!" Hoss muttered.

After a time Rimrock leaped down. "You just stay there," Hoss warned. "You got away with it one time, but— Whoa!"

Rimrock was in the air, coming up all the way from the ground this time. He landed on the sheepskin and crouched there, looking well pleased with his achievement.

Hoss was still shaken. "Watch that!" he yelled. If Rimrock set one claw into Paiute by accident. . . . "And get your fat tail away from his flank!"

All the way back to the cabin Rimrock played at the new game. With all the tremendous springy power of a cat he landed on the sheepskin every time, but he could make a slip, Hoss knew.

The worst of it was, now that he had learned the feat, he would try to come aboard when Paiute had no protection over his hide. Hoss could just see himself standing on his head in a rock pile, with Paiute on his way out of the country.

Hoss did something about it. The next day he

made a thick pad of old blankets and deer hide. He wet the hide and shaped it to fit Paiute, and then he sandwiched it between the other material, hair-side down for extra padding. When the hide dried out, it offered flinty protection against Rimrock's claws.

Lacing the whole thing together with rawhide strips, Hoss rigged the pad so it would stay in place behind the saddle.

During construction Rimrock showed great interest in the project. He ran off with the deer hide, jumping and snarling and dragging it along—until he stepped on it and went rolling end over end. Hoss caught him then and gave him a few cuffs where it did the most good.

The lion learned that he was not to attempt to get on Paiute until the pad was in place. The twelve-hundred pound horse didn't mind the extra burden in the least. Long before, he had accepted Rimrock as a privileged inhabitant of the line camp. In the days that followed, the horse began to stop on his own when he saw Rimrock waiting on a rock or stump near the trail, holding steady until he felt the lion land on the pad.

Hoss was rather proud of the accomplishment. He felt like one of the Tartar khans he had read about, riding around the country with a lion. He seemed to remember that he had seen a lion ride on the back of a pony in a circus when he was little. He didn't think it had been a mountain lion, though. He doubted that anyone had ever accomplished as much with a mountain lion as he had with Rimrock. The only trouble was, he couldn't show off before anyone or even brag about it.

Oh, yes, Rimrock was a fine rider, but he still wasn't developing any ability to catch anything except rabbits. Having repaired his rifle stock as best he could with rawhide and baling wire, Hoss was still in the deer business to keep Rimrock fed.

Every evening when Hoss marked the calendar, he had a bad moment. The time was flying. Instead of doing anything to get rid of Rimrock, he was making the lion more dependent every day.

And Rimrock was getting bigger every day.

Years before, back in the cedar breaks country, there had been an old hermit called Plato who lived in a rock cabin with all kinds of birds and animals as friends. Old Plato had a pet lion that he had raised from a cub. Like Rimrock, the lion always whisked away whenever a stranger showed up.

Cowboys were a little wary about going near Plato's cabin because of that lion, but every now and then someone rode up to take the old man some food and to see if he was all right.

And then one day Sam Hargis' father found Plato dead and pretty well torn up. Everyone assumed it was the lion that had done it, and there was a great to-do about his turning into a maneater. The whole country turned out for a lion hunt, with three professional hunters bringing in dog packs.

After one day everyone but the professionals tired out, though some of the hunters stayed in the hills for a few days, telling lies to each other and having a good time. The real lion hunters went on and got three or four big cats and a couple of cubs, and then everything cooled down.

Hoss thought about that as he sat in the cabin looking at Rimrock.

He was sure that Rimrock was a rare exception to the big cat family, because he had tamed so easily and was so good-natured. But it was still a fact that a full-grown mountain lion was about as savage and unpredictable as any wild animal in the world. The Lord just hadn't intended them to be tame.

The time Hoss had given himself to do something about Rimrock slid away so fast that he shook his head helplessly one night when he marked the calendar and saw that he had only two days left.

There was no use waiting out those two days; he'd just as well go back to the Ponderosa in the morning. It had been a bad mistake to take the extra time with Rimrock. Now he was fonder of the lion than ever.

The real mistake, he thought bleakly, had been made the day he hadn't had the heart to kill a helpless cub.

Hoss closed the line camp the next day. He used the table to board over the window solidly. Rimrock would have to understand that he had no refuge inside any longer.

Since he knew the lion would follow him as far as the flats, no matter what he did, Hoss let Rimrock take his last ride on Paiute. At the bottom of Old Mine Hill, when he saw they were headed into open country, Rimrock jumped off and waited in the trees.

Hoss untied the pad and threw it away. Angry at himself and circumstances, he yelled, "We're through! Go back where you belong and stay there!"

He rode out on the flats. Rimrock came to the edge of the trees, and then he ventured a short distance from cover, but the long-stretching open plain was too much for him. He retreated, padding

along in the trees, seeking to find some way to stay close to Hoss without having to go out on the bleak, exposed flat.

There was no way, of course, for the rider was going straight away from him, getting smaller all the time.

It was a poor ending, Hoss thought, but it was all he could do. The five-mile width of flats just might be the barrier that would separate them for good, but even if Rimrock crossed the plain by night, he would soon start running into all kinds of strange things: cattle, horses that he had never seen before, roads, wagons, strange odors and noises—all kinds of activity that should scare him back to the hills.

Most likely, though, Rimrock wouldn't take a chance on the flats, even by night. He would go back to the cabin and hang around there until it finally soaked into his head that he was a wild animal, that there was no one around any longer to skin his rabbits for him.

Why, even house cats often reverted to the wild state in a short time. After a week of having to provide for himself, Rimrock probably would be well on his way to forgetting that he had ever known a man.

8

The Ponderosa

It was good to be home again. The well-built stables and corrals and the huge, solid ranch house of the Ponderosa were a welcome contrast to the little one-room cabin Hoss had occupied most of the winter.

Ben Cartwright, a blocky, gray-haired man with a strong, confident appearance and manner, welcomed his son heartily. Then he wanted to know all about the cows.

"I wouldn't say they got fat up there digging grass out of the snow, but they came through all right."

As was not uncommon at the Ponderosa, there were visitors who were going to stay the night. Hoss knew one of them, Mel Stark, a Virginia City livery stable employee, a young, good-looking man who was quite a fancy dresser away from the stable.

He had been driving a cattle buyer around to various ranches in a buggy. The buyer, Mr. J. T. Orton, was a middle-aged, portly man who wore a derby hat and a heavy, gold watch chain across a brocaded vest.

At supper that night the conversation between Pa and Orton showed that Orton no doubt knew his business well when it came to cattle buying. He worked out of Omaha, Nebraska, traveling over a large part of the West, and he was full of interesting tales of his experiences.

Hoss saw Little Joe grin slyly when Orton got on the subject of lions. It was a subject Hoss didn't care about in the least at the moment, but Orton had been talking to Sam Hargis two days before.

"I've heard those big cats will crouch on a tree limb over a trail and drop right down on a rider before he knows what's happening," Orton said.

"Did Sam Hargis tell you that?" Pa asked.

"No, no! All he did was complain about how he's been losing calves. No, I was told that story back in Kentucky one time. Back there, they call lions panthers or 'painters.' "

Pa nodded. "Panthers, cougars. . . . Their real name is puma. We just call them mountain lions out here."

"Will they drop out of a tree on a man?" Orton asked.

"I've never heard of it happening." Pa gave Little Joe a warning look to keep him from making some wise remark. "To tell the truth, Mr. Orton, I've never heard of a case in this country of a mountain lion bothering a man, unless, of course, he was wounded."

"The lion or the man?" Little Joe asked.

Orton laughed, but it was obvious that he had a fear of wild animals.

"What about old Plato?" Stark asked.

"That was an unusual case." Pa told the cattle

buyer about the hermit. "Any kind of full-grown wild animal kept right in the house would naturally be dangerous."

The conversation was making Hoss uneasy. He kept watching Little Joe, wondering how much his brother might have guessed about Hoss's real reason for staying on at line camp.

"I only heard about Plato, of course," Stark said. "I wasn't in the country when it happened, but I do know that back in Tennessee, where I come from, panthers were known to tackle human beings every now and then."

"I just never heard of any such thing out here," Hoss said, unable to keep still any longer. "Another thing, I've always been convinced that lions get the blame for a lot of killing they don't do. Bears can really tear up a bunch of calves, and wolves are even worse."

Immediately Orton wanted to know about the dangers of encountering bears, and whether they would attack human beings.

"Bears are not so bad," Little Joe said. "You can generally wrestle them, and if you tickle them good right behind the fourth rib—"

"Joseph!" Pa gave his son a stern look, and then he apologized to Orton. "He sometimes has an unusual sense of humor."

Hoss was relieved when the talk turned back to cattle.

Pa told Orton that he had a herd he would be interested in selling, and that they could ride out to look at it in the morning.

"I can't tomorrow, Mr. Cartwright, because I've made arrangements to meet Mr. Holcolmb at his ranch, and then I have to go to two other places, if everything works out during the next few days. If it's all right with you, I'd rather come back here in three or four days."

"That's fine," Pa said. "The boys and I have about three good days' work putting the new hay lift in the barn."

"I knew I should have stayed in line camp," Hoss

groaned. "Here I was figuring on going to town and—"

"A few more days won't make any difference," Pa said. "I'm paying storage on a warehouse full of hay in town, so I want that new lift in as soon as possible."

Little Joe made a face. "No use, Hoss. I think that girl married somebody and moved to San Francisco last winter. You see, I told her you liked it so well in line camp that you'd decided to spend the rest of your life there."

"If I'd known you were going to be just as smart-alecky as ever, I just might have stayed."

Orton smiled, but his mind was never very far from business. "If I can rent a horse from you, Mr. Cartwright, I can let Stark go on back to town. I think I know the country well enough now to get around."

"We have nothing to rent, but we sure can lend you a horse. I think—"

"I hate to say this, but I'm not much of a rider.

Me and horses just never seemed to get along too well. If you have a real gentle one. . . . Do you?"

Pa nodded. "I think we can find one to suit you. Little Joe will take care of you in the morning. I believe Geronimo will be suitable for you, Mr. Orton."

"Geronimo?" The cattle buyer showed alarm. "That has a real mean sound."

"Gentle as a daisy," Little Joe said.

Orton wasn't convinced. He looked to Pa for assurance, and Pa said, "I'm sure Geronimo will be fine."

Later in the evening, while the others were talking and having coffee in the living room, Hoss was deep in the story of Marco Polo, reading again how the khans rode with leopards behind the saddle. He thought it was a doggone shame that he would never be able to make anyone believe that he had done the same thing with a mountain lion.

There were a lot of things about Rimrock that no one would ever believe. It made him feel a little guilty to think of the lion *browring* around the cabin, hungry and lonesome, waiting for Hoss to come back.

Little Joe said, "That's the first time in years I've seen you with your nose in a book. What are you reading?"

Hoss turned several pages quickly so his brother could not see *where* he had been reading, at least. "I don't figure to be ignorant all my life, like some people."

They were still bantering when Orton paid Stark for his services. Little Joe pursed his lips in a soundless whistle and indicated with his eyes the fat sheaf of bank notes the cattle buyer took from his coat.

"I'd suggest you have me put that in the safe tonight, Mr. Orton," Pa said. "While we're fairly law-abiding out here most of the time, we do have our problems now and then."

Orton smiled. "All right. I have my fears, I'll admit, but being robbed was never one of them, strange though that may sound."

On his way to the kitchen for a drink of water about ten minutes later, Hoss heard the horses in the corral snorting, and then he heard the sound of hooves striking the stalls in the barn. He tried to seem unhurried and not unduly alarmed as he turned back through the living room. "Sounds like a horse is acting up. I'll go see about it."

Stark rose quickly. "It's that half-broken buggy mare, I'll bet." He followed Hoss out into the darkness.

At least one horse in the stable was trying to kick his stall to splinters. Hoss ran as soon as he was outside, and clutching him was a fear he did not want to admit.

As Stark had thought, it was the buggy mare that was raising the devil, although the other horses were nervous, too—all except Paiute. Hoss lit a lantern, and then he and Stark together got the animals quieted.

"That's funny," Stark said. "The one you rode in today don't seem to be upset."

"Paiute? It takes a wolf or some other wild animal to scare him."

"That's what I mean. The rest of them act like they'd smelled a bear." Stark went outside. A few moments later Hoss heard him shout excitedly.

He ran out to where the man was standing behind the stable.

"I saw a lion, Hoss!"

"Aw, what are you talking about!"

"I did, I swear! Just the other side of that fence. It went toward those trees."

"Bobcat."

"No, sir! It was too big for that."

From the doorway of the house Pa shouted, "What's going on out there?"

"Nothing!" Hoss answered. "Some little old animal."

"It wasn't little," Stark insisted. "It looked pretty big to me, Hoss."

"About ten feet long, huh?"

"No. . . . Not anything like that, but it was

shaped like a lion and—"

"So's a bobcat, Stark, and if you want to get right down to it, so's a house cat."

"I know, but—"

"Did you get a real good look at it?"

"Well, no. I just had a glimpse, but still—"

"Who ever heard of a lion being down this far?"

"I'll admit it would be pretty unusual," Stark said.

"You're doggone right it would."

Stark nodded. "I guess so. It *must* have been a bobcat."

Hoss thought he had convinced the man, and then Stark reached for the lantern Hoss was carrying. "Let's go find the tracks."

Hoss swung the lantern away from the reaching hand. "What in tarnation for? That Chilton family that stayed here last summer raised chickens, or tried to, and ever since then the bobcats have been coming back to look around."

"Yeah. They sure got a taste for chickens, all

right." Stark followed Hoss back to the stable. He laughed suddenly. "Wouldn't that throw a scare into old Orton, if we went back inside and said we'd seen a lion?"

The horses were all right now. Hoss blew the lantern out and hung it up. *Rimrock, get out of here,* he prayed. *Clear out of here and hit for the hills.*

They went back to the house. "It was a bobcat prowling around," Stark said.

"How big do *they* get?" Orton asked quickly.

Pa had to stifle a smile, while Little Joe was on the verge of giving some outrageous answer, but Pa got his lick in first. "They're not very large, Mr. Orton. Nothing to worry about at all."

For a man who had been all over the West, the cattle buyer sure didn't know much about wild animals, Hoss thought.

Hoss didn't sleep very well that first night at home. After being in line camp so long, he found his bed too soft, and the house seemed stuffy. He got up and opened the window and stood for a while looking out over the porch roof at the dark outbuildings and the tall trees beyond.

That doggone Rimrock. . . . Clear across the flats. He must have started at dusk or soon afterward. The things that Hoss had thought would drive him back apparently hadn't bothered him at all.

There was still one thing that Hoss could do. He had thought about it before, but he didn't like the idea one bit. He could send Rimrock to a zoo or a circus.

He remembered the mangy, half-starved animals he had seen in circuses in Virginia City. Crowded into small, filthy cages, hauled for hundreds of miles through dust and heat. That would save Rimrock's life, or at least prolong it for a while, but it would not be much of an existence for any animal.

No.

Before he would do that to Rimrock, he would shoot him. But he would do that only as a last resort. Maybe Rimrock already had had enough of civilization. Maybe he was headed back to the hills right now.

Hoss tried to convince himself that it was a bobcat that Stark had seen.

But he was sure that it was not.

9

Nocturnal Visitor

LONG BEFORE Hop Sing, the Ponderosa cook, was up and preparing breakfast, Hoss was out beyond the barns and stable busily trampling out lion tracks with his size fourteen boots. He did not find very many of them near the buildings, and in the trees beyond, where the dead leaves were still on the ground from the fall before, he found none at all.

After breakfast he saw Stark going over the same ground. "No use looking," Hoss called to him. "It was a bobcat, all right. I saw a track or two earlier."

"I don't see anything now but your tracks."

"I must have messed them up."

Little Joe was in the yard with Geronimo, the gentlest horse in the Ponderosa string. "Did I ever tell you about the time Hoss tramped out the tracks of fifty steers just walking along behind them after his horse got away? When it comes to feet—"

"I'll show you what I can do with one of them feet, if you don't shut up," Hoss threatened, and Little Joe laughed.

Carrying his carpetbag, Orton came out of the house with Pa. "I guess I'm as ready as I'll ever be," Orton said, looking at Geronimo with disfavor. "That's the horse, huh?"

"He'll give you no difficulty, Mr. Orton."

The cattle buyer wasn't so sure about that. He walked around Geronimo twice, studying him for some evidence of an evil, violent nature. Pa lashed the carpetbag on behind the saddle. "There's nothing to worry about. Why, a child would be safe on Geronimo."

"That's just the trouble; I'm not a child, Mr. Cartwright."

Little Joe laughed, and Pa gave him a sharp look.

After a time Orton girded up his courage and mounted. Nothing happened except that Geronimo sighed. The rider looked down at the ground. "My, he's sort of tall, isn't he?"

"Those long legs make him a good walker," Pa said.

"That's all I intend to do—walk him."

"Give him a loose rein," Little Joe advised. "You can even loop the reins over the horn and let him go, if you want to."

Orton started out of the yard slowly. "I'll be back in three or four days, Mr. Cartwright."

The Cartwrights watched Orton go around the corner of the stable and out of sight. Hoss and Little Joe looked at each other, shaking their heads and grinning.

Stark left soon afterward in the livery buggy, going back to Virginia City.

"Now that you boys have had your laugh, let me tell you something," Pa said. "Mr. Orton is not quite the tenderfoot he makes himself out to be. Oh, he's no broncobuster, I'm sure, but neither is he as big a greenhorn as he acts."

"What's the idea, then?" Little Joe asked.

"The idea is that about the time some people decide he doesn't know much about cattle, either, they'll suddenly wake up to the fact that they've sold a herd to him for about two dollars a head less than they figured on."

Little Joe grinned. "He didn't fool me a bit."

Pa took his gloves from his hip pocket and put them on. "Let's go to work."

They worked until dusk building scaffolding in the huge hay barn, the first step toward installing a new overhead trolley and hoist for storing baled hay in the tremendous loft.

By the time he went to bed, Hoss realized that he had not done very much in line camp to keep himself in shape. But he knew that the never-ending chores around the Ponderosa would soon take care of that little problem.

He hardly stirred during the night. At breakfast the next morning no one mentioned any disturbance among the horses. Hoss considered that good evidence that Rimrock had got his belly full of civilization with one visit.

By now he was undoubtedly back at line camp—and hungry enough to be performing like a proper mountain lion.

His muscles stiff and sore after another day's hard work in the hay barn, Hoss was sleeping soundly that night when he dreamed that he was back in line camp, with Rimrock walking on him to wake him up.

He sighed and started to roll over.

The dream was very real. Something really was putting weight on him. He woke up with a start.

"You!"

"Browr," Rimrock said happily and licked Hoss's cheek with his sandpaper tongue.

Jumping out of bed, Hoss accidentally kicked a chair halfway across the room. It made a fearful racket—and a most painful impact against his big toe. He groaned and sat down on the bed, holding his foot. Rimrock rubbed against him.

After a while, having decided that his toe was not broken and that the noise of the chair hadn't roused the whole house, Hoss picked Rimrock up and started toward the window with him.

"Back the way you came. Across the roof and down the tree," he ordered the cub in a whisper.

But Hoss didn't shove the lion out, for he realized that it would not do any good. If he put him out and closed the window, Rimrock most likely would stay on the porch roof, probably scratching at the window the rest of the night.

No, it was better to let him stay. He would leave at first light, anyway.

That would not solve the problem, but at least it would give Hoss a little more time to think of something. He realized that he had been giving himself "just a little more time" for months, and nothing had come of it—and here he was back in the same old rut.

"Do you want to be shipped to a zoo?" he whispered. He felt Rimrock's lank stomach. "You haven't been eating much lately, have you?" Hoss put the lion down. "Now don't go bumping into things and making a racket."

The door squeaked a little on its hinges as Hoss opened it. He had never noticed that before. He stood in the hall, listening. Little Joe's room across the hall was quiet.

Every board in the hall and every tread on the stairs seemed to creak loudly as Hoss eased his weight down on his bare feet. Crossing the living room, he bumped his sore toe and barely restrained a loud grunt of pain. He crept through the kitchen and on into Hop Sing's ice cellar.

There was a huge roast on the chopping block. Rather than risk staying too long to cut off a part of it, Hoss took the whole thing and started to sneak back upstairs.

Little Joe had been half-waked by the sound of the chair in his brother's room. He was almost sound asleep again when he heard Hoss going downstairs, but that was nothing unusual. After a man spent several months in line camp, it took him a while to get used to sleeping in the house.

Maybe Hoss was after a drink of water, or going out to get some air before he tried to sleep again. Or maybe the bobcat had scared the horses. Little Joe almost slipped off into deep slumber. And then he heard the odd scratching noise from somewhere upstairs.

Maybe that was Orton— No! There were no visitors in the house. The noise persisted, but Little Joe was too sleepy to care. Once more he started to doze off, and then he heard Hoss coming back upstairs.

What was going on, anyway? Still not fully awake, Little Joe rose and opened his door. He saw his brother's huge form coming along the hall.

"What's all the racket about?" he muttered.

His voice startled Hoss, who stopped and put his hands behind him quickly. "Nothing, nothing. Go on back to sleep."

"What have you got there?"

"Just a snack."

"Oh!" Little Joe almost closed the door. He was leaning against the casing with one eye half-open, ready to turn and stagger back into bed, when he saw Hoss continue on by holding a fifteen-pound chunk of meat. Old Hoss sure did have an appetite.

Little Joe lurched over to the bed and tumbled in. A moment later something jerked at his mind. He sat up suddenly. Snack? Raw meat?

Still partly sleep-confused and groggy, he went across the hall and opened the door to Hoss's room. Hoss was sitting on the bed in his nightshirt. What looked like a monstrous, long-tailed dog was crouched on the floor near him, eating the big piece of meat.

"What . . ." Little Joe mumbled.

"Rimrock. I'm just feeding him. You see—"

"No place for a dog." Little Joe closed the door and turned to go back to his room. Then for the first time he came completely awake. That had been a mighty odd-looking dog!

He whirled around and opened the door and went inside. "That's no dog! That's a—a— Oh, my gosh!"

Rimrock ran under the bed.

"A—a—lion!" Little Joe gasped.

"Be quiet! Don't wake Pa. I'll explain everything."

Little Joe walked around the foot of the bed. Afterward he thought he must not have been fully awake, after all, or he wouldn't have gone into the room. "What are you doing with a lion?"

"Shh! Dad-burn it, you'll wake Pa!"

It was then that Rimrock, frightened by the strange presence and voice, scrambled from beneath the bed and leaped through the doorway into the hall.

"Look what you did!" Hoss groaned.

They heard Rimrock thumping down the stairs.

"I don't want Pa to know about this!" Hoss wailed.

"Don't want him to know! Why, he's going to be eaten up in a minute."

"Rimrock won't hurt anything. He's a pet." Hoss grabbed his brother's arm. "You got to help me get him out of the house."

"I favor that, all right, but—"

"He won't hurt you. Come on!" Hoss flew out of the room with his nightshirt flapping and fluttering behind him.

"You don't have to drag me," Little Joe whispered. "I'll go, but I don't know why."

Little Joe was right behind his brother when they reached the dark living room. Everything was quiet, and they could see nothing of Rimrock.

"You open the front door, while I go back by Pa's room," Hoss said.

Hoss felt his way in one direction, while Little Joe started for the front door. A moment later Little

Joe fell over a chair and grunted heavily. Hoss heard the noise in Pa's room as Pa jumped out of bed.

"Get that door open!" Hoss said hoarsely.

A few seconds later Little Joe said, "I got it."

"Did he go out?"

"I don't know whether he went out or another one came in. Doggone you, Hoss—"

"What's going on in there?" Pa yelled.

"Nothing!" Hoss answered, and then he started across the room. "Where is he?"

"I don't know. That's what I'm worrying about."

An instant later they both knew where Rimrock was. Pots and pans rattled in the kitchen. Dishes tumbled to the floor. A light bloomed suddenly back there, and then Hop Sing began to yell wildly in Chinese.

The last crash was a big one. Hoss knew that Rimrock had gone through the window.

With a pistol in one hand, a lamp in the other, and his hair on end, Pa came charging into the kitchen just after Hoss and Little Joe got there. The place was a mess. Hop Sing was jumping up and down, waving a lamp in one hand and a butcher knife in the other.

"That bobcat!" Hoss said. "How'd he get in here?" He gave little Joe a jab in the ribs with his elbow.

Hop Sing recovered his English. "Lion!" he screeched. "Velly big lion!"

"Aw, it couldn't have been," Hoss said.

Paw stepped on a broken dish with his bare foot and grimaced in pain. "What's going on here?"

"Well, Pa, the best I can figure is that the old bobcat Stark saw the other night—somebody must have left the front door open and. . . ." Hoss spread his hands.

"Lion!" Hop Sing howled.

"Now, what would a lion be doing in the house?" Hoss asked.

"Big lion! Velly long tail!" Hop Sing gestured to show what he meant, and the butcher knife swept close to Pa's nose. Pa grabbed the cook's wrist and took the knife away from him.

"Put that lamp down before you set the house on fire." Pa glared at Hop Sing. "You saw the lion?"

Hop Sing nodded vigorously. He spoke rapidly in Chinese.

Pa scowled at Little Joe. "And you say you saw a bobcat?"

"I heard it. Hoss saw it."

"Lion!" Hop Sing insisted. "Velly fellocious! Big tail!"

"Yes, sir, Pa, that old bobcat sure went out through that window," Hoss said.

"I flighten him!" Hop Sing said.

"Something doesn't make sense here." Pa studied his sons and the cook with suspicion. "Hop Sing, did you ever see a lion before?"

"See one tonight! Velly big. Long tail."

Pa shook his head. He was angry, disgusted, and confused, and he had cut his foot on the broken dishes. "If the door was open, why didn't he go out the way he came in?"

Hoss shrugged. "You know how wild animals are when they get in the house."

"I *don't* know! I'm not accustomed to having wild animals in the house."

Hop Sing plucked a few strands of tawny hair from the edge of the broken window. He waved it under Pa's nose. "See? Big fellocious lion hair, you bet!"

"Bobcat fur, I swear," Hoss said.

Pa waved his hands. "That's enough for tonight. Everyone get back to bed, and you, Hoss, make sure that the front door is closed. I don't see how it could have been open in the first place."

"I close *my* door, you bet," Hop Sing said. "Big—"

"All right! Everyone go to bed." Pa looked at his injured foot. "Bobcats . . . lions. . . . What are we running here, anyway?"

Little Joe followed Hoss into his room when they went upstairs. "Let's hear about this two-hundred pound bobcat of yours."

"Aw, Rimrock won't weigh fifty pounds, hungry

as the poor little thing is—maybe less."

"Yeah, that was what I was thinking when I was down there in the dark—just how hungry he was."

Hoss sat down on the bed. "I shot this old mother lion a few months ago, see? The cub was up a tree, a little spindly tree that would hardly hold a squirrel. I put my sights on him, and then. . . ." Hoss began to rub his sore toe.

"He was so cuddly and cute, you just couldn't do it?"

"That's right, doggone it! So I carried him back to line camp." Hoss shrugged. "After a while, when he got so tame and all. . . . Well, there you are."

"Here you are, you mean, with a great big, fat problem on your hands. You're an old mother lion, that's what!"

"It ain't funny, Little Joe!"

"It sure won't be when Pa finds out you made a pet of a mountain lion, right in the same camp with his herd of prize cattle." Little Joe grinned. "It'll make you awful popular with all the ranchers in the country, too. Have you ever thought of moving to San Francisco, or maybe Paris?"

"Aw, shut up." Hoss sighed. "You've got to help me."

"How can I help you? I'm the one who scared the lion downstairs and clean through a window. To tell the truth, it was a question of whether he was going out first or me. About one more minute in the dark down there, with everything quiet, and *I* might have gone through a window. You know where I was just before he got out? I was on top of the safe and wishing it was fifteen feet higher."

"He wouldn't have harmed a hair of your head."

"It wasn't my hair, it was my neck I was worrying about."

"I'll tell you how you can help me. We've got to stick to the bobcat story."

Little Joe indicated the partly eaten piece of meat on the floor. "You think Hop Sing won't be telling Pa plenty when he sees that roast is gone from the ice cellar?"

Hoss made a wry face. "Maybe Hop Sing won't miss it."

"Ha! He'll miss it, all right, and then you'll have to explain how the bobcat opened the cellar door."

Hoss groaned. "We'll just have to wait and see what happens." He tried to find a happy thought. "Maybe Rimrock is gone for good. What with all the fuss, getting scared, and trapped in the house—"

"Any lion that will follow you across five miles of open country, where no self-respecting lion would be caught dead, is not going to give up. Oh, he'll return. You're the only family he's got, Hoss."

"Maybe I ought to go tell Pa the whole truth right now." Hoss stood up.

"Go ahead."

"In the morning." Hoss sat down.

"You sure?"

"No."

Little Joe went to the door. *"Meerowr,"* he said, grinning. "Of course, you know what that means. That's lion talk for good night, old mamma cat."

10

The Killing

In the morning Hop Sing still insisted that he had seen a very ferocious lion. Hoss stuck to the bobcat story. Though he knew it was past time to tell the truth, he kept hoping that the whole thing would blow over. Oddly, Pa no longer seemed interested in questioning his sons and Hop Sing about the disturbance.

That was a bad sign in itself, Hoss knew. Pa was just waiting for him to hang himself high.

Before they went to work in the hay barn, they all looked outside for tracks. Apparently Rimrock had approached the house from the back, leaving no tracks in the dead leaves, and he must have departed by the same route after crashing through the window.

Pa made no comment, but his quiet, thoughtful look left Hoss and Little Joe feeling uneasy. Hoss had got rid of the roast by throwing it from Little Joe's bedroom window, as far back in the trees as he could hurl it. As far as Hoss knew, Hop Sing had said nothing about the disappearance of the meat.

Again the Cartwrights worked all day in the hay barn. They finished installing the hay lift and tested it. Now all that was left to do was to remove the scaffolding. Pa said nothing more about the uproar in the house the night before, and Hoss and Little Joe were quite willing to let the subject lie.

After supper Little Joe asked his brother, "If your little friend comes back tonight, then what?"

Hoss had been worrying about that very thing all day.

"If he does, the first thing you don't do is to let him out of the room."

"Don't worry. I won't even let myself into your room."

Just before dusk Hoss said he was going to the stable to currycomb some of the long winter hair from Paiute. He intended to make at least a pretense of doing so, but he couldn't find his favorite currycomb, the one with the extra-large grip that fitted his hand.

It didn't matter, anyway. He stalled around for a while and then he went out the back door of the barn and walked into the trees, looking for Rimrock. He knew that if the lion was anywhere close and saw him alone, he would surely come to him.

He took a long walk through the trees, and when he was far enough from the house not to be heard by Pa, he called to Rimrock, but he neither heard nor saw anything of the lion. That scare in the house might really have cured him of ever wanting to go near a human habitation again. Hoss tried to picture him loping across the flats in the dark, heading for where he belonged as fast as he could. It was a comforting thought, but somehow Hoss could not make it stick convincingly in his mind.

He would not have been surprised if Rimrock had walked out from behind a tree at any moment.

It was well after dark when Hoss returned to the house. Pa was working on his books. He didn't even glance up to ask Hoss why it had taken so long to currycomb a horse.

Little Joe asked a question with his eyes, and Hoss shook his head.

Restless during the night, Hoss woke up several times, thinking he had heard Rimrock on the porch roof. Twice he rose and looked out, but there was nothing to indicate that the lion had ventured near the house.

He must be pretty doggone hungry, Hoss thought. If he hadn't gone back to the hills, he was probably trying to catch something to eat.

The Cartwrights had just finished tearing down the scaffold the next morning when Sheriff Roy Coffee rode into the Ponderosa with shocking news.

"That cattle buyer, Orton, was killed last night about six miles from here, just this side of Indian Pond." Coffee swung down and stretched his legs. "I've been riding half the night, and now I've got to go on back to town to check on a thing or two there."

He declined Pa's offer of coffee. "If I go in and sit down, Ben, I'll be there a half hour."

"How did it happen, Roy?" Little Joe asked.

"Well, he left the Halstead place about noon yesterday. He was headed back here. Right there in the trees near the pond something jumped him."

"What do you mean?" Hoss asked.

The sheriff brushed his hand across his dusty, grizzled moustache. "All the sign points to a lion, if you can believe that."

"That's crazy!" Hoss said.

Coffee nodded. "That's what I said when I first heard it. Some prospectors with a wagon found him last night about six o'clock. They'd seen some lion tracks in the road a short time before, and then they found Orton all scratched and clawed up under a tree. They loaded him in and hauled him to town."

"He was dead then?" Pa asked.

Coffee nodded. "I got there just at daylight and scouted around some. There were some lion tracks down the road a piece, sure enough."

"What about where they found him?" Hoss asked.

The sheriff scrubbed dust out of his mouth and spat disgustedly. "By the time those prospectors got through tromping around, there wasn't much of anything to see, but they swore there was a lion track or two when they first found him."

Little Joe and Hoss exchanged glances, and then Little Joe looked at the ground.

"What about the horse?" Pa asked.

"He ran back toward Halstead's place. One of Halstead's riders picked him up early this morning." Sheriff Coffee frowned. "There's a long streak of claw marks on his rump. Orton's carpetbag was still on him."

"Orton was carrying a lot of money, Roy," Pa said slowly.

"So I hear. In a wallet in his coat, according to Halstead."

Pa nodded. "That's the way he went out of here with it."

"A darn fool habit, if you ask me, but I guess he'd been doing it right along." Coffee paused. "There was no money on him when the prospectors found him."

"There you are!" Hoss said. "No lion killed him, but somebody is trying to make it look that way. How about those prospectors?"

"You're jumping at things, Hoss," the sheriff said. "Sure, they could have taken his money after they found him, or anyone else that might have happened along that road, but I've got no way of proving that. You just can't guess at these things, you know.

"If they were trying to make out that a wild animal killed him, it don't seem reasonable they would have tromped out all the sign and then hauled the man into town." The sheriff shook his head slowly.

"So you say it was a lion that did it?" Hoss asked.

The question irritated Coffee. "I said it looks that way. I'm keeping tab on those prospectors, don't worry. Doc Inman is out of town, so I don't have a report from him yet to be real sure about the cause of death. It might even have been a bad heart. Say a lion did take a whack or two at him, why, he could have died from just being scared."

Hoss was pretty well scared himself. "You find where Orton's money went, and you'll find the man who did it."

The sheriff studied Hoss keenly. "Maybe."

"Don't worry about Roy doing his job." Pa gestured toward the house. "Sure you won't have some coffee with us?"

"Not today, Ben. Thanks." Coffee got on his horse. "By the way, the town was pretty excited last night after those prospectors came in. They'll probably have a big lion hunt stirred up by tomorrow. Sam Hargis has been figuring on it for some time, anyway, and I guess he's already sent for Curly Joe and his dogs."

Coffee waved and rode away. Hoss stood looking at the ground. Rimrock wouldn't kill anyone. Doggone, he just wouldn't do a thing like that! No doubt his tracks were everywhere by now, but that was no proof that he'd jumped Orton.

And now, all excited over the killing, ranchers and town loafers—anyone who had a horse and gun—would be swarming over the countryside looking for a lion. With a dog pack on his trail, Rimrock would have no chance at all in a land of rolling hills and trees. They would have him in no time, once the dogs picked up the scent.

"Hoss," Pa said.

Startled from his gloomy thoughts, Hoss looked at his father's stern expression with misgivings.

"We had some kind of wild animal in the house night before last. Among other mysterious things he did, he opened the door to the ice cellar and took a roast that Hop Sing had all ready for the next day."

"He did?" Hoss said weakly.

"It's time for the truth. Let's have it."

"I was going to tell you." Hoss looked at Little Joe. "Yes, sir, I intended to right along, but I just didn't get around to it."

"I'm waiting."

"Well, it *was* a lion in the house the other night. Just a little old lion, Pa, hardly worth mentioning."

"Let me judge that. Go on."

"His name is Rimrock. I sort of made a pet of him up at line camp, and I reckon he must have followed me home."

Pa's mouth fell open. "You made a pet of a lion cub? A man who grew up with horses and cattle? Are you standing there telling me you deliberately made a pet of a mountain lion?"

"Yeah." Hoss looked to his brother for help, but no aid was forthcoming there. Little Joe was easing away toward the hay barn. "Yeah, I reckon I did."

"Just a minute there, Joseph!" Pa rapped. "You aided and abetted in that bobcat story, so don't try to sneak away!"

"Oh, I wasn't, Pa. I was— I was— Yeah. . . ."

"Come on, Hoss; let's have the story."

"There's nothing much to tell. I raised him from a cub. He stayed in the cabin with me, and he used to follow me over to the herd—"

"You took him to the herd?"

"He sort of followed me, at first. Oh, he didn't bother the cows. He's afraid of them."

"I imagine."

"He really is, Pa. Whenever I got close to the herd, Rimrock would jump off and—" Hoss guessed he could have said something else besides that.

"Jump off what?" Pa demanded.

"Paiute."

"What! You mean to tell me you carried a killer lion on a horse?"

"He rode behind me. I had a pad fixed for him."

Pa's outraged look was enough to curdle milk, but Hoss saw no reason to stop now. He went right on telling about some of the things he had taught Rimrock, and how gentle and affectionate the lion was. "I know what you're thinking, Pa, but it isn't right. He wouldn't have bothered Orton or anyone else. He was always shy around strangers. He was even afraid of strange horses. Why, he always—"

"All right, all right!" Pa raised his hands. "So he's a paragon of gentleness, but who's going to believe that when they see him? And how do you really know that he didn't try to jump on Geronimo, just looking for a ride?"

Hoss shook his head violently. "He wouldn't have done it! I told you he's afraid of horses, except Paiute."

"Maybe he suddenly lost that fear," Pa said quietly. "Something clawed that horse, and something killed Orton."

"It wasn't Rimrock," Hoss said stubbornly.

"How do you know? He was hungry—you said so yourself. He was down here in a strange country, wild and scared, and"—Pa pointed his finger—"he's a mountain lion. No matter what you say, he's a wild animal, one of the most treacherous of all his kind. He's fair game to the first man that sees him."

"Nobody's going to see him. I'm going to find him and take him back to the hills."

"Oh? And if he killed Orton, you're still taking him back to the hills, eh?"

"He didn't kill anybody!"

"Maybe not, but we never can be sure about that. You can't find him just to turn him loose, Hoss." Pa's gaze bored into his son. "You're going to find him, all right, but you're going to shoot him."

"No."

"Yes."

"He saved my life when I was snow-blind."

"And now he may have taken one, so the score is even."

"I won't shoot him."

"I will," Pa said angrily. "If I ever lay eyes on him, I'll shoot him."

"You ain't going to get the chance." Hoss wheeled around and went into the stable to saddle Paiute. He heard Little Joe talking earnestly to Pa, and Pa was still angry. He glared at Hoss when he led Paiute from the stable. Hoss looked at him levelly.

"You'd better do as I say, Hoss!"

"Not this time, Pa. I know I'm right." Hoss rode away.

After two hours of fruitless search, he began to wonder if he was right. It didn't seem possible that Rimrock would have turned into a savage killer overnight, but the fact remained that mountain lions were highly unpredictable.

Hoss turned west and rode to Indian Pond. He found the place where Orton had been killed, under a huge ponderosa pine beside the road. Sheriff Coffee certainly was right. There wasn't much to be seen there now of tracks that would help untangle the mystery. The prospectors had messed things up, to begin with. Then Coffee had walked all around the place, and on top of that, two or three riders had been there after he left. Probably some of Halstead's cowboys, Hoss guessed.

He wasted little time there, but went on looking

for Rimrock, riding the thickets and the groves of trees. Late in the afternoon he returned to the Ponderosa from the east, having made a big circle. He was in a bleak, discouraged mood when he tramped over to the house after putting Paiute in his stall.

Pa and Little Joe were waiting for supper in the living room.

"No luck, huh?" Pa asked, and Hoss could tell by the tone that he was no longer angry.

Hoss shook his head. "I never even saw a track."

"Maybe he finally lit out for the mountains," Little Joe said.

"I hope so."

"Si Brenneman came by while you were gone," Pa said. "The country is in an uproar, sure enough. There'll be thirty, forty men here tomorrow morning, along with Curly Joe and his dogs."

"What am I going to do? The whole thing is my fault. If I hadn't tamed Rimrock so he depended on me. . . . He won't have a chance against those dogs. Once they get a whiff of his trail, he'll be treed in a half hour. It won't be like up there in the rocks."

"There's not much you can do," Pa said.

"I can't let them go out there and—"

"Wait a minute." Pa was sympathetic but firm. "You can't stand against the whole country in this thing, Hoss, especially when every man in that bunch of hunters is going out fully convinced that a lion killed Orton."

"Do you really think Rimrock killed him?"

"I don't know, but what I think doesn't mean a thing. You know how people feel about lions."

"Yeah, I know," Hoss said. "I guess I felt the same way before I ran into Rimrock. You just don't know how different he is. Just let me tell about when I was snow-blind. . . ."

Pa and Little Joe listened to the story with keen interest, glancing at each other now and then.

When Hoss had told it all, Pa was silent for a while. "I can see how that makes it all the tougher for you now." He hesitated. "But you still can't buck the whole country when they go out on a lion hunt."

"I reckon not. If I could only find him. . . ."

"The fact that you couldn't find him sort of indicates that he cleared out, doesn't it?" Little Joe asked. "If he had been hanging around, he would have come to you when you were out riding, wouldn't he?"

"I thought so." Not finding Rimrock was a hopeful sign, Hoss decided. He felt a little better when they went to supper.

Hop Sing made one comment during the meal. "No more roast-stealers come, huh?"

In spite of all of Hoss's wishful thinking, Rimrock had not gone back to the high country. In the middle of the night he approached the Ponderosa silently from the west side of the house, leaped lightly into the tree that stood close to the porch roof, crouched on the roof for a few moments looking all around the dark yard—and then slipped through the open window.

His return was the last thing Hoss had expected.

He didn't know that Rimrock was there until he started to turn over and felt the weight against his feet.

"Well, I'll be doggoned!" Hoss reached down and rubbed the lion's head. Rimrock stretched out luxuriously.

Moving swiftly then, Hoss rose and closed the window. He lit the lamp and looked Rimrock over carefully. The lion *browred* contentedly and closed one eye as Hoss scratched his lopped ear. The man felt his stomach. "So you finally learned to catch something to eat, huh?"

Rimrock rubbed against his legs, and then he jumped back onto the bed. "Oh, no! You and me are going to take a ride."

Hoss opened his door a few inches and yelled for Little Joe to get up.

After a time Little Joe peered cautiously into the room, opening the door just wide enough to see in with one eye. "Oh, oh! *Now* what are you going to do?" he demanded.

"Look at him," Hoss said. "Do you think a little old thing like him would kill a man?"

"I can't judge those things very good in the middle of the night, and I'm not coming in to find out."

"Go saddle Paiute for me. Take one of those heavy tarps in the barn and fold it into six thicknesses and tie it good behind the saddle, and then bring the horse right up to the front door."

"Who's going to hold the horse while you walk up to him with that monster?" Little Joe asked.

"You won't have to hold Paiute. Just stay way back, so Rimrock won't get nervous."

"You can bet I'll do that, all right!"

After a while Little Joe returned to report that the horse was ready, and then he retreated quickly down the stairs. All the lamps in the living room were lit when Hoss entered it carrying Rimrock in his arms. The front door was wide open. Pa and Little Joe were standing at the entrance to the back hallway, while Hop Sing was peering around the edge of the kitchen doorway with a cleaver in his hand.

"Velly fellocious roast-stealer!" Hop Sing observed. "Look out, Hoss!"

The spectators made Rimrock uneasy. He tried to wriggle out of Hoss's arms on the way across the living room.

"Don't anybody come outside," Hoss warned.

Pa had lit the porch lamps, so there was plenty of light outside. Those in the house watched from the windows.

Hoss had a few bad moments when, ready to mount, he put Rimrock down. The lion scooted off into the darkness and it seemed that he was gone, but Hoss kept calling to him and he came back. Paiute reached down and smelled noses with the lion.

Watching through the window, Pa shook his head in disbelief.

Hoss swung up. Rimrock crouched on the ground. "All right, you big knothead, jump!"

In an effortless, graceful leap Rimrock went up on the canvas pad, digging his claws in and settling down with his long tail tucked in and his head close to Hoss's side.

"I don't believe it," Little Joe muttered.

Pa shook his head. "I'm not so sure I saw it, either."

"Me saw!" Hop Sing said.

"When the hunters get here tomorrow, you didn't see anything. Understand?" Pa said.

Hop Sing grinned. "Saw no roast-stealer. Saw nothing!" He gestured with the meat cleaver and Little Joe ducked.

Hoss reached the hills a half hour before dawn. Rimrock leaped down then and went into the trees. He came back when he saw that Hoss had stopped.

"This is as far as we go together, Rimrock. It's the end of things for us two. Don't you understand? From now on, whenever you see a man—any man—you've got to hide. I know it's my fault that you're the way you are, but now you've got to change. . . ."

It was no use, Hoss knew, but he talked to Rimrock anyway, telling him what he must do to save his life. The man stayed until light broke clearly on the long flats. Rimrock was prowling around somewhere back in the trees then.

He would not cross the flats in daytime, Hoss was sure. He probably could not even be coaxed to ride across them on Paiute.

As he rode away quickly Hoss wondered how many times he had done the same thing before, each time hoping the separation would be final. He saw Rimrock bound from the trees and come out a short distance on the flats and then return to cover.

Run for the rocks. Run for the rocks.

11

Caught!

THERE WERE ALMOST fifty in the posse of lion hunters that rode into the Ponderosa not long after Hoss returned from his trip. Some of the riders clearly showed the effects of a pre-hunt celebration in Virginia City saloons. They would be more dangerous to each other than to anything they chased.

Curly Joe's eight dogs were pacing restlessly in a big cage on a light spring wagon, eager to start the hunt. Curly Joe was a tall man in greasy buckskins, with dark hair that hung to his shoulders.

Sam Hargis was directing the hunt. "You Cartwrights ready, Ben?"

"We're ready." Pa had told Hoss that he didn't have to go, but Hoss was going. "Where do you figure on turning the dogs loose, Sam?"

"Curly Joe says there's no use to uncage them before we cross the flats. He says it's unlikely that the lion that got the cattle buyer stayed this low for more'n a day."

That was jarring news to Hoss. He had figured that Curly Joe would start the dogs somewhere close to where Orton had been killed. Instead of helping Rimrock, he had taken him where the dogs would pick his scent up quickly.

Hargis started to say something else, and then one of the tipsy hunters fired a pistol and shouted at the top of his voice.

"Stop that shooting!" Hargis yelled angrily.

"Let's go!" someone yelled, and Hoss saw that it was Mel Stark, the livery stable employee.

He kept thinking about Stark as he rode away beside Pa and Little Joe. The hunters spread out wide to avoid each other's dust, some of them yelling and laughing and making a great holiday of the occasion.

"You had no way of knowing that Curly Joe would take the dogs clear to the hills before starting," Pa said.

Hoss shook his head glumly. "I never seem to do anything right."

Most of the cavalcade passed on the east side of Indian Pond. A few went around the west side, riding the brush on the off chance that a lion was there. They had plenty of time for small, private hunts, since the wagon hauling the dogs was much slower than the horsemen.

"Did you see the sheriff in this bunch?" Hoss asked.

Little Joe shook his head. "I didn't see him."

Hoss stopped suddenly. "I'll catch up later." He turned Paiute back toward Indian Pond. Little Joe hesitated, on the verge of following his brother.

"No," Pa said. "Don't you see? He doesn't want to be in at the kill. To tell the truth, after last night

I haven't got much stomach for it myself."

Hoss left Paiute under the tree where Orton had been killed. There was a big overhanging branch about twelve feet up, about right for a lion to crouch on. Just too doggone right, Hoss thought, just what anyone might think would be a perfect ambush place for a lion.

To the east of the tree, a gentle slope ran down to the pond. West of it was thick brush and timber. Hoss made his search in that direction. He found the tracks of a man, who apparently had done the same thing he was now doing. Coffee, no doubt.

In ever-widening circles Hoss kept searching, until he began to wonder if he was merely wasting time. The sheriff would have looked everything over thoroughly. And then, under a tall tree with a thick needle mat below, Hoss found a spot where a horse had stood for some time.

He almost missed the sign, since the needles had been brushed over the marks. It was the yellow spots against the bark that led him to the place, marks left by the breaking off of small dead limbs. On hands and knees he pawed through the needles. There was no doubt that a horse had stood here, and someone very cleverly had hidden the sign afterward.

Still on hands and knees, Hoss saw something in the brush about fifteen feet away. He retrieved it, staring at it in astonishment.

His favorite currycomb!

It was a tool stamped out of metal, with wedge-shaped teeth. Five of the teeth had been pulled away from the backing until they were a half inch long, and then they had been sharpened with a file. All the other teeth had been hammered down.

Dark, dried stains showed what the currycomb had been used for.

Hoss put his suspicions together rapidly. The thing to do now was to take them to Sheriff Coffee. No, he would do even better than that; the man who had killed Orton and put the blame on a helpless little lion was riding with the hunters.

He took four long steps before the voice stopped him.

"Too bad you found it, Hoss."

He whirled to face Stark, who had stepped out from behind a tree with a pistol in his hand.

"Drop your gun belt, Hoss."

Hoss had no choice but to obey. "You think that lion story is going to fool anyone?"

"It did pretty well—until you got to nosing around. Now you know what I've got to do, don't you?"

Hoss estimated the distance between them. It was too far, but once he got started, he would close it mighty fast. He flexed his hands.

"Don't try it!" Stark warned.

He would catch at least one bullet, Hoss knew, before he reached Stark, but if he could just get his hands on the man for thirty seconds, it might be worth it. Tense with anger and a desire to lunge toward Stark, Hoss almost took the chance, and then common sense asserted itself.

Hoss studied the man narrowly. The pistol was steady enough, but Stark's eyes betrayed a nervousness. He was the kind who would shoot quickly and go right on shooting. In fact, it was a wonder he hadn't done so already.

Stall, Hoss thought. *Talk to him. Try to get closer.*

"You knew it was a lion that night at the Ponderosa, didn't you, Stark? You pretended to let me talk you out of it."

"That doesn't matter now. Turn around, Hoss, and walk slow. You and me are going down to the pond."

So that was it, Hoss thought. The pond. A bullet in the back, and then a rope and a big rock. The north end of the pond was plenty deep.

"No. I'm not going anywhere with you, Stark."

Stark raised his pistol carefully, sighting.

"You'd better make the first one real good, but it won't stop me. I'll get to you before I go down. You just bet I'll get there, Stark, and then I'll tear you apart! I mean it!"

Hoss saw the man's eyes waver. A coward was never sure of himself.

"There's a way out of this," Stark said. "I need five or six hours' start. Give me that and I'll let you go. I don't really want to shoot you. You know that."

Hoss wasn't about to believe a word he said, but he played for time. "How do you figure to work that?" He gestured with his hands, and at the same time he eased forward a little.

"Hold it! Don't try that, Hoss!" Stark was tight and scared; he would pull the trigger the instant he thought he was threatened. He licked his lips slowly. "I'll tell you how. We'll go down to the pond and I'll tie you up and take your horse with me. By the time you get loose and walk to the Ponderosa, I'll be well on my way."

The pond. Stark couldn't get it out of his mind. Hoss would never walk anywhere if he went down there with Stark. "You're sure you'll just tie me up, huh?"

"I promise. It's a way out, Hoss. You and me

have always got along fine, haven't we?"

"Yeah, I guess so," Hoss said slowly, as if he were giving serious consideration to the proposal. "You did kill Orton, didn't you?"

"I didn't say so. All right, let's go down to the pond."

"I want to be sure—"

"You've stalled enough. Turn around."

Maybe he'd get a chance on the way to the pond, Hoss thought, a quick dive into the brush—something. . . . But he saw from Stark's expression that the man was following his thoughts. Hoss made his decision. If there was any chance at all, it was right now.

He set himself to drive in at Stark.

And then the harsh command came from the trees. "Drop it!" Hoss saw Sheriff Coffee step into the open behind Stark.

Stark whirled and fired. He was an instant late and his shot was wild. The sheriff's bullet caught him in the right arm and spun him around. His pistol fell from his hand, and a moment later Hoss landed on him at the end of a running leap, smashing him to the ground.

Then Coffee was shouting at Hoss, beating at his arms. "I want him in one piece!"

Hoss got up, shaking his head to clear it. "I guess I *was* a little mad, Roy." He watched Coffee pick up Stark's pistol. "What are you doing here, anyway?"

"What am *I* doing here? What are *you* doing here? You doggone near messed things up good and got yourself shot in the bargain!"

"I— Well, you see, I thought—"

"I know what you thought! You had the idea I was so old and dumb I couldn't catch a cheap killer. You thought I swallowed that lion story right from the first. I'm not so blind that I can't read sign about as good as any man. I found that currycomb where he'd lost it the day I was scouting around here."

"You did?" Hoss mumbled.

"Of course I did! But I wasn't dumb enough to pick it up and carry it away. I knew if he worried about it long enough, he'd sneak back and try to find it."

"You mean you knew it was Stark all along?"

"No, I mean I suspected him. I've been having him watched in town, and then yesterday when Doc Inman told me Orton was killed with a knife—" Coffee shrugged. "It all fit together."

"I didn't know, Roy."

Coffee's good nature began to return. "It's all right, since you didn't get killed." He pulled Stark to his feet and looked at his wounded arm. "You'll live. Where'd you hide the money?"

"What money?"

"Never mind. I already found it—right there behind the boards in the livery stable."

Stark's defiance crumpled then. "It wasn't right for him to have all that money, and me—"

"Shut up!" Coffee rasped. "Give me a piece of your shirt to wrap his arm, Hoss. And then get his horse." He pointed. "It's over there about two hundred yards."

Twenty minutes later, Sheriff Coffee rode away with his sullen prisoner, while Hoss went on to join the hunters. It just might slow down some of them, at least, when he told them about Stark. Anything at all that he could do to help Rimrock. . . .

While he was still on the flats he heard the distant baying of the dogs and he knew by the tone that they were hot on a fresh scent. He pushed Paiute as hard as he dared.

The sound of the dogs was even more distant when he overtook the first group of hunters in the rough country west of Mora Creek. They were dismounted, giving their horses a rest.

"Where's the main bunch?" Hoss asked them quickly.

One of the men, a barroom loafer from Virginia City, shook his head. "The dogs jumped something over east of here, when we first hit the hills. There was a lot of shooting, and then everything got mixed up. It sounded like the dogs were going in all directions."

Hoss told them about Stark.

"I never did think a lion done that killing," a man said. He looked sourly at the rough country ahead. "This is pretty mean work."

"It gets a heap meaner, the farther you go. You'll be walking most of the time from here on," Hoss said.

"Not me," the man said.

At the foot of a high, rocky ridge, Hoss caught up with another group of hunters. The dogs were still far ahead, baying excitedly, while the hunters were studying the ridge, wondering how to get up it without walking.

"There's a way around," Hoss said, "but it's a long haul and you have to walk some of it."

"Yeah." One of the hunters shook his head. "And by that time, the dogs will be another ten miles away, and over four more ridges."

Hoss didn't bother to tell them about Stark; he

could see that they weren't going to last much longer, anyway. "Did any of you boys see a lion when all the shooting was going on?"

"I did," a man said. "About half-grown, he was. He was moving like the devil was nipping his tail."

"Did anyone hit him?"

"Not as far as I could tell. He didn't give us much to shoot at."

Hoss rode back to the east to get around the ridge. Four of the hunters followed him. Two of them quit when they came to the next ridge and saw what lay ahead, and then one more dropped out when Hoss dismounted and said there was nothing but climbing left.

Slim McCrea, the Hargis rider, stayed with him. They climbed toward the sound of the dogs.

12

Treed Lion

PART WAY UP the ridge, McCrea stopped and gasped, "I don't see how you move all that weight so fast."

Hoss was heaving and panting. While they were resting, they suddenly heard a frenzied note in the baying of the dogs. Rimrock was treed!

"Let's go," Hoss said.

It was a lung-bursting climb to the top. Still ahead of them was another ridge, and it was from beyond it that the sound of the dogs was concentrated. To their disgust, they saw riders coming up the back side of the ridge they had just climbed, men who must have gone a long way to find an easy ascent.

Among them were Pa and Little Joe and Hargis.

"Where's Curly Joe?" yelled Hargis at Hoss.

"I haven't seen him since we left the Ponderosa."

"There was some kind of mix-up down there where we first jumped the cat," Hargis said. "Joe was blowing that cow horn of his and yelling like sixty, and then he fell behind, and we don't know what happened to him."

"We'd better wait for him," Hoss said.

"What for?" Hargis motioned for McCrea to get on behind him. "We've got a treed lion, and that's good enough for me."

"Wait a minute, Sam." Hoss told them about Stark.

"Good for Coffee!" Hargis said. "Now let's go get our lion."

Pa shook his head at Hoss, once more telling him there was nothing to be done about Rimrock. Hoss rode double with him.

"I'm sure it's your lion," Pa said. "I got one good look at him down in the timber."

It was only a short distance before they all had to dismount for the final climb over the ridge. Looking back, Hoss saw Curly Joe coming on his mule, still a long way off.

Hargis saw him, too, but he was not going to wait for anyone. He pulled a rifle from the boot on his saddle. "There's Joe, but I reckon we don't need him now for what's left to do."

Sick at heart, Hoss took Pa's rifle, and Pa gave him a long, understanding look.

Hoss was one of the first to reach the top. The dogs were below on the north slope, milling around a huge yellow pine tree. They were biting at the tree bark, howling, snapping at each other, jumping against the tree—wild with excitement.

"There he is!" McCrea yelled. "There on that big limb about halfway up."

Hoss took a quick look at the tawny form half-hidden by the needle clusters of the limbs. End of the trail for Rimrock. It seemed only yesterday that he had first seen the lion, a furry little lop-eared

cub trying to cling to a tiny branch during a snowstorm.

Someone raised a rifle.

Hoss knocked it down. "You fool! At this distance you'd likely only wound him."

Pa put his hand on his son's shoulder. "Easy, Hoss."

Hoss led the way down the ridge. One thing he knew for certain. It was going to be a clean, merciful shot. He would do it himself.

The others fell behind as he charged recklessly down the slope, plunging between the rocks, leaping from one slab to another, scrambling over the rough granite without regard for skin or clothing.

"Slow down!" Hargis yelled.

Hoss stopped when he was a short distance from the tree. He could see the lion clearly then. Ears back, teeth showing white in a snarling face, it was crouched on a limb, looking down at the frantic dogs.

It was not Rimrock, but a full-grown lion!

Little Joe came up beside Hoss. "Hey! That isn't him, is it?"

"Nope, it sure isn't."

"Hold it!" Hargis shouted at someone, but his order went unheeded.

One of the hunters, almost as excited as the dogs, fired hastily with a pistol. The heavy bullet struck the lion and jarred him badly. Hoss raised his rifle to finish the job, but the lion scrambled back to the trunk and put it between himself and the hunters.

Needle clusters fell. The dogs leaped around to the far side of the pine. The big cat was coming down, losing his grip on the bark, sliding to the ground below.

An instant later he fell among the dogs and immediately there was a savage, snarling bedlam. One dog went spinning end over end, howling in mortal pain. Another crawled away with his stomach ripped open. The savage struggle wound up in a thick growth of serviceberry bushes, with dust and twigs and fur flying in all directions.

Wounded though he was, the lion put up a tremendous fight. Working in cautiously on the rocks, the hunters were unable to take a shot for fear of hitting one of the dogs. Three times Hoss raised his rifle, and then lowered it again, afraid to shoot into the threshing tangle.

The same man who had wounded the big cat let his excitement carry him away a second time. He fired and killed a dog.

It ended when Curly Joe, white with rage, dashed down the slope and went right in with the dogs and killed the lion at point-blank range with a pistol shot. And then his anger made everyone turn away or stare at the ground.

"You gutless idiots!" he said in a cold, level voice. He called the whole group seven different kinds of fools—and other names. He swore to kill the man who had dropped a wounded lion among his dogs. "Hargis, I told you to hold everything until I showed up, in case of a treeing."

Hargis was a tough man to buffalo, but he took it. "I know you did, Joe. I'm sorry about—"

"Who wounded that cat?"

"We don't know. Somebody lost his head, I guess."

"I'll blow it off for him! Who was it?"

"How could anyone tell in all the excitement and yelling?"

"Weak-brained coyotes, the whole bunch of you! Look at Old Blue. Look at Growler, there." It was only when he turned his attention to the injured dogs that Curly Joe began to cool down. Three of them were dead, and it looked to Hoss that a fourth was fit only to be shot.

That was the one with the ripped stomach. Curly Joe gave it attention first. From a big flap pocket under his buckskin shirt he produced needle and thread and began to sew up the dog.

The Cartwrights and Hargis and McCrea stayed to give any help they could. The other hunters slipped away quietly.

"It looks pretty bad," Hoss said. He was holding the dog for Curly Joe.

"He's got over far worse than that," the lion hunter growled. "What idiot wounded the cat?"

"I don't know," Hoss said.

"I'm sorry about this," Hargis said. "I'll pay you for the dogs, or whatever I can do."

"Money!" Curly Joe shook his head. "You think money can replace a good dog?"

Hargis shrugged. "That's all I can do."

Hoss, too, was sorry about the whole affair, the dead and injured dogs, the torn figure of the lion lying in the bushes—the entire mishandled ending.

He carried one of the injured dogs back to the horses. Curly Joe carried the other one. He had come prepared for trouble, for he unrolled two large panniers from behind the saddle on his mule and looped them over the crosstrees. They put the injured dogs in them and Curly Joe walked away without another word, leading the mule.

"We'll trail along with him, McCrea and me,"

Hargis said. "I feel kind of bad about this. Where's your horse, Slim?"

"I hate to think of where it is."

"I'll bring it in for you," Hoss offered. "I'll meet you at Dutch Springs in about an hour, say."

Instead of mounting, Hargis led his horse, and he and McCrea walked down the ridge after Curly Joe and his mule.

Pa looked out over the vast broken country to the aspen thickets far below. "There ought to be room here for us all for a while yet—men and cattle and the wild animals that were here first—even lions."

Hoss and Little Joe were silent, looking at the wild free run of land in all directions from the ridge.

"I saw your lion down there, I'm sure," Pa said. "The dogs must have chased him right across the trail of that big cat. Maybe he'll get a chance to grow up now, Hoss."

"Yeah. I reckon he'll have as much chance as any

of his kind, and that's all I hoped for." Hoss sighed heavily.

Pa picked up the reins of his horse. "We'll meet you down at Dutch Springs with the others."

It was slower climbing down the ridge than it had been coming up, but Hoss was in no great hurry now. Curly Joe was mad enough at Hargis and everyone else in this part of the country that he might not work it for lions for a long time, and that would give Rimrock a chance to learn a few things he needed to know.

Hoss reached the horses and mounted wearily, taking McCrea's sorrel in tow.

It was hardly ten minutes later that he saw Rimrock. The lion was crouched on a slab of rock against a cliff, looking down at him.

"Oh, my gosh! Now if he follows me home again. . . ."

Hoss thought of shooting close to him to scare him. He almost yelled at him in anger, to tell him to get out, for all the good that it would do.

And then he put Rimrock to the test.

"Come here! Come down here, you jughead!" he shouted.

Rimrock left the slab, leaping down where the man could not see him, and Hoss thought, "What a dumb thing I did. Now I've got him on my hands again."

But the next time he saw Rimrock, the lion was going up, headed back toward the high, rocky country. Hoss shouted again and Rimrock went a trifle faster.

It had come home to him at last, the dogs, the trampling horses, the yelling and the shooting—the terror of being pursued by man. He was going where he belonged.

Hoss jerked his rifle free and emptied it against the rocks a hundred feet or more away from the lion. *Run, Rimrock, run. Know that every man in the world is against you from now on. Never show yourself to man, but run and hide and live your life as you were born to live it.*

After the first shot, Hoss saw no more of Rimrock, but he sat for several minutes looking up at the rocks, and his expression was a curious mixture of sadness and relief.

Whitman ADVENTURE and MYSTERY Books

Adventure Stories for GIRLS and BOYS...

REAL LIFE STORIES

- To Dance, To Dream
- The Great War
- Heroes in Blue and Gray

POWER BOYS SERIES

- The Haunted Skyscraper
- The Flying Skeleton
- The Burning Ocean
- The Million-Dollar Penny
- The Double Kidnapping

DONNA PARKER

- In Hollywood
- At Cherrydale
- Special Agent
- On Her Own
- A Spring to Remember
- Mystery at Arawak
- Takes a Giant Step

TROY NESBIT SERIES

- Forest Fire Mystery
- Indian Mummy Mystery
- Mystery at Rustlers' Fort

New Stories About Your Television Favorites...

I Spy

Lassie

- Secret of the Summer
- Forbidden Valley
- Wild Mountain Trail

The Man from U.N.C.L.E.

Combat! The Counterattack

The Beverly Hillbillies

The Munsters

- The Great Camera Caper
- The Last Resort

Gilligan's Island

The Big Valley

Bonanza

Voyage to the Bottom of the Sea

Walt Disney's Annette

- Mystery at Medicine Wheel
- Mystery at Moonstone Bay
- Mystery at Smugglers' Cove